Richard Jago

Poems

Moral and Descriptive

Richard Jago

Poems
Moral and Descriptive

ISBN/EAN: 9783744716284

Printed in Europe, USA, Canada, Australia, Japan

Cover: Foto ©Andreas Hilbeck / pixelio.de

More available books at **www.hansebooks.com**

POEMS,

MORAL and DESCRIPTIVE.

BY THE LATE

RICHARD JAGO, A.M.

(PREPARED FOR THE PRESS, AND IMPROVED BY THE
AUTHOR, BEFORE HIS DEATH.)

TO WHICH IS ADDED,

SOME ACCOUNT OF THE

LIFE AND WRITINGS OF MR. JAGO.

———

LONDON:

PRINTED FOR J. DODSLEY, IN PALL-MALL.

MDCCLXXXIV.

THE CONTENTS.

A 3   *To*

SOME

SOME ACCOUNT

OF THE

LIFE AND WRITINGS

OF

MR. *JAGO*.

THE life of a country-clergyman, conſtantly engaged in the duties of his profeſſion, and the practice of the domeſtic virtues, however reſpecta ble ſuch a character may be, can afford but ſlender materials to the biographer. But Mr. JAGO being here exhibited to the Public as an Author poſſeſſed of a

con-

confiderable fhare of poetical merit, fome account of him may be expected, and cannot be uninterefting to thofe, who, it is prefumed, will be pleafed with his writings.

The Family of Mr. JAGO was of Cornifh extraction : but his father, the Rev. RICHARD JAGO, was rector of Beaudefert, in Warwickfhire. He married MARGARET, the daughter of WILLIAM PARKER, Gent. of Henly in Arden, 1711, by whom he had feveral children. RICHARD JAGO, the author of thefe Poems, was his third fon, and born the 1ft of October 1715. He received a good claffical education un-

der

der the Rev. Mr. CRUMPTON, an excellent country fchool-mafter, at Solihull, in Warwickfhire; where he formed an acquaintance with feveral gentlemen who were his fchool-fellows; amongft others, with the late WILLIAM SHENSTONE, Efq; with whom he correfponded * on the moft friendly terms during life. From fchool he was entered of Univerfity College, Oxford, where he took his degree of Mafter of Arts, 9th July 1738, having taken orders the year before, and ferved the curacy of Snitterfield, near Stratford-upon - Avon. In 1744 he married

* See SHENSTONE's Works, Vol. III.

DOROTHEA

DOROTHEA SUSANNA FANCOURT, a daughter of the Rev. Mr. FANCOURT, of Kilmcote in Leicefterfhire; to which living Mr. JAGO was fome years afterwards prefented.

For feveral years after his marriage he refided at Harbury, to which living he was inftituted 1746. At a fmall diftance lay Chefterton, given him much about the fame time by Lord WILLOUGHBY DE BROKE; the two together amounting to about 100 l. a year. Before his removal from that place, he had the misfortune to lofe his amiable companion, who died 1751, leaving him a numerous family of fmall children;

dren; and, from such a lofs, the moft inconfolable widower.

In 1754, Lord CLARE, (now Earl NUGENT,) who had a great regard for him, by his intereft with Dr. MADOX, Bifhop of Worcefter, procured him the vicarage of Snitterfield, where he had formerly been curate; worth about 140 l. a year : whither he removed, and where he refided the remainder of his life.

In 1759 he married a fecond wife, MARGARET, the daughter of JAMES UN-DERWOOD, Efq. of Rudgely, in Stafford-fhire; who furvived him.

Mr.

Mr. Jago was prefented in 1771, by Lord Willoughby de Broke, to the living of Kilmcote, before mentioned; worth near 300 l. a year, and refigned the vicarage of Harbury.—During the latter part of his life, as the infirmities of age came upon him, he feldom went far from home. He amufed himfelf at his leifure, in improving his vicarage-houfe, and ornamenting his grounds, which were agreeably fituated, and had many natural beauties.

Mr. Jago, in his perfon, was about the middle ftature. In his manner, like moft people of fenfibility, he ap-

peared

peared referved amongft ftrangers :
amongft his friends he was free and
eafy ; and his converfation fprightly
and entertaining. In domeftic life, he
was the affectionate hufband, the tender parent, the kind mafter, the hofpitable neighbour, and fincere friend;
and both by his doctrine and example,
a faithful and worthy minifter of the
parifh over which he prefided. After
a fhort illnefs, he died on the 8th of
May 1781, aged 65 years, and was
buried, according to his defire, in a
vault which he had made for his family in the church at Snitterfield. He
had children only by his firft wife;
three fons, who died before him, and

four

four daughters, three of whom are now living.

To do juſtice to Mr. Jago's charac-ter as a poet, would require the pen of a more able writer, than the compiler of theſe memoirs. It may ſafely be aſ-ſerted, however, on the authority of the public approbation, which they have already met with, that the pieces on which we reſt Mr. Jago's poetical fame, viz. his Poem of *Edge-Hill*; his Fable of *Labour and Genius*; and his *Elegies*, on the Blackbirds, &c. are all excellent in their kind.

The poem of Edge-Hill, though the ſubject

subject is local, and chiefly descriptive, yet Mr. JAGO has contrived to make it *generally* interesting by his historical narrations, and digressive episodes; and by his philosophical disquisitions or moral reflections, particularly the philosophical account of the Origin of Mountains, which is equally curious and poetical. His description of the Earl of LEICESTER's Entertainment of Queen ELIZABETH, at Kenelworth-castle, which is truly characteristic of that pedantic age: as the moral reflections on the ruins and departed grandeur of that superb structure, is in the best manner of YOUNG, in his Night-Thoughts.

The

The ſtory of the Youth reſtored to
Sight, from the Tatler, is told with ſo
many natural and affecting circum-
ſtances, as makes Mr. Jago's *poetical*,
much ſuperior to Sir Richard Steele's
proſe narration.

The hiſtorical account of the important Battle of Kineton, or Edge-
Hill, contains ſome curious facts, not
generally known, as well as very ſuita-
ble reflections, religious and moral, on
the fatal effects of civil diſcord.

The Fable of *Labour and Genius*,
the ſubject of which was ſuggeſted by
Mr. Shenstone, is told with ſome humour,

mour, and great clearnefs and precifion;
with a very ufeful moral forcibly in-
culcated.

As for the Elegy on the *Blackbirds,*
we need no other proof of its merit,
than the violent inclination which fome
perfons have difcovered, unjuftly to ap-
propriate to themfelves the credit of
that performance.

When it firft appeared, with Mr.
JAGO's name to it, in DODSLEY's Mif-
cellanies, a manager of the Bath theatre,
with unparalleled effrontery, boafted in
the circle of his acquaintance, that *he*
was the author of it; and that JAGO

was a fictitious name which he had adopted, from the celebrated tragedy of OTHELLO.

But I was more astonished to find lately, that the excellent Biographer of our English Poets, in his life of GILBERT WEST, should leave this affair still dubious; when it is demonstrable from the very letters of Mr. SHENSTONE, to which Dr. JOHNSON refers, that Mr. JAGO was the real author.

The case seems to have been thus. As Mr. SHENSTONE was fond of communicating any poetical productions of his friends, which he thought would

do

do them credit; he probably gave a copy of Mr. JAGO's Elegy to the LYTTELTON family at Hagley, where Mr. WEST frequently vifited. And as Mr. WEST thought it worthy to appear in Dr. HAWKSWORTH's Adventurer, he might fend it to him without mentioning Mr. JAGO's name, which was then very little known in the world. So that Dr. HAWKSWORTH might well imagine, that Mr. WEST himfelf was the author of it, as Dr. JOHNSON has hinted. However this may be, there is happily a living evidence, who is able and ready to fupport indifputably Mr. JAGO's claim to this beautiful elegy; as well as to the others of the *Swal-*

lows,

lows, and *Goldfinches* ; in all which Mr. JAGO's original genius appears, and in which, as THOMSON fays, he has

———— ——— ——— ——— " touch'd

" A theme unknown to Fame, the paffion of the

" Groves."

The poem of Edge-Hill, &c. are here re-printed, as they were corrected, improved, and enlarged by the Author a fhort time before his death, with fome additional pieces which now make their firft appearance, in particular the Roun-delay written for the Stratford Jubilee, which is beautifully expreffive and cha-racteriftic of SHAKESPEARE's verfatile ge-nius,

nius, and multifarious excellence—All which are fubmitted to the candour of the Public, by their obedient

Humble fervant,

Tʜᴇ EDITOR.

H I N T S

F O R A

P R E F A C E

F O R A N Y A U T H O R,

A N D

F O R A N Y B O O K.

THE following sheets were fairly tran-
scribed, the title page was adjusted, and
every thing, as the writer thought, in readi-
ness for the press, when, upon casting his
eyes over them for the last time, with more
than usual attention, something seemed wanting, which after a short pause, he perceived

to be the *Preface*. Now it is fit the reader
fhould know, as an apology for this feeming
inattention, that he had formerly rejected
this article under a notion of its being
fuperfluous, and uninterefting to the reader;
but now when matters were come to a crifis,
and it was almoft too late, he changed his
mind, and thought a preface as effential to
the figure of a book, as a portico is to that
of a building.

Not that the author would infinuate by
this comparifon, that his paper edifice was
entitled to any thing fuperb and pompous
of this fort; but only that it wanted fome-
thing plain, and decent, between the beg-
garly ftyle of Quarles, or Ogilby, and the
magnificence of the profufe Dryden. Far be
it from him, by calling this fmall appendage
to his work by the name of a portico, or
an antichamber, or a veftibule, or the like,

to

to raife the reader's expectations, or to en-
courage any ideas but thofe of the moft
fimple kind, as introductory to his fubfe-
quent entertainment : neither would he, like
fome undertakers in literary architecture,
beftow as much expence on the entrance,
as prudently managed, might furnifh the
lofty town apartments, or paftoral villa of
a modern poet. On the contrary, he referves
all his finery of carving and gilding, as well
as his pictures, and cabinets for their proper places within.

But for the further illuftration of his
meaning he chufes to have recourfe to allu-
fions more nearly related to his fubject, fuch
as the prelude to a fong, or the prologue to
a play, there being evidently a great affinity
between rhiming and fidling, writing verfes,
and playing the fool.

Another confideration which greatly in-
fluenced

fluenced the author in this point, was, the
refpect which he bears to the Public.   For
conceiving himfelf now in the very act of
making his appearance before every circle of
the polite, and learned world, he was ftruck
with awe, and felt as if he had been guilty
of fome indecorum, like a perfon abruptly
breaking into good company with his hat
on, or without making a bow.   For though
by his fituation in life he is happily reliev'd
from any perfonal embarraffment of this
kind, yet he confiders his book as his proxy,
and he would by no means have his proxy
guilty of fuch an impropriety as to keep
his hat on before all the learned men of
Europe, or to omit making his bow upon
being admitted to an audience, or prefented
in the drawing-room.

Great is the force of this little article of
gefticulation, from the loweft clafs of ora-

tors

tors in the ſtreet, to thoſe in the higheſt de-
partments in life; inſomuch that it has been
thought, a prudent, attentive, and ſkilful
manager, either on the ſtage, or at the bar,
as well as the bowing Dean in his walk, may
acquire as much ſucceſs, amongſt polite, and
well-bred people, and particularly the ladies,
who are the beſt judges, by the magic of
his bow, as by any other part of his action,
or oratory.

Yet, notwithſtanding all that the author
has ſaid concerning this external mark of
reverence, he is ſenſible that there is a ſet
of cynical philoſophers, who are ſo far from
paying it due regard, that they count it no
better than a refined ſpecies of idolatry, and
an abomination utterly unbecoming ſo noble
and erect a creature as man. Upon theſe gentlemen it is not to be expected that the beſt
bow which the author, or his book could
make,

make, would have any effect; and therefore
he fhall decline that ceremony with them,
to take them by the hand in a friendly manner, hoping that they will make fome allow-
ance for his having been taught againft his
own confent to dance, and fcribble from his
infancy.

He is aware likewife that there is
another fect of philofophers, whom his ingenious friend Mr. G. author of the Spiri-
tual Quixote, diftinguifhes by the name of
cenforious Chriftians, " who," as he expreffes
it, " will not fuffer a man to nod in his
elbow-chair, or to talk nonfenfe without
contradicting or ridiculing him."—But as
the writer of this admirable work has fhewn
himfelf fo able, and fuccefsful a cafuift in a
fimilar inftance of a petulant, and over officious zeal, he hopes thefe gentlemen will, in
imitation of Mr. Wildgoofe, for the fu-

ture

ture refrain from a practice fo injurious to
their neighbours repofe, and fo contrary to
all the laws of civility and good manners.

It is true, fome of thefe literati may be
confidered under a more formidable character, from their cuftom of holding a monthly
meeting, or office for arraigning the conduct
of all whom they fufpect of maintaining
heretical opinions contrary to their jurifdic-
tion. In this view thefe good fathers fcru-
ple not to put an author upon the rack
for the flighteft offence, and not content
with their claims of infpiration and infalli-
bility, will torture his own words to prove
his guilt. In the execution of this office
they judge all men by their own ftandard,
and like the tyrant PROCRUSTES, regardlefs
of the acute pain they inflict at every ftroke,
will lop off a foot, or any other portion of
an author's matter, or lengthen it out, as

beft

beſt ſuits their purpoſe, to bring him to their meaſure.

But to the inexpreſſible comfort of him-ſelf, and of every free-born Engliſh writer, the author reflects that the competence of ſuch a court cannot be admitted in a pro-teſtant country; and to ſpeak the truth, from experience, its power, as exerciſed amongſt us, though ſtill very tremendous, is tem-pered with a gentleneſs, and moderation un-known to thoſe of Spain and Portugal.

But though the author is not without hopes, by his complaiſance, and conde-ſcenſion, to conciliate the affections of all thoſe various ſects of the learned in every part of the world, yet his principal depen-dance is upon the gentle, and humane, whoſe minds are always open to the feelings of others, as well as to the gratification of their own refined taſte, and ſentiments; and

to

to thefe he makes his appeal, which he
hopes they will accept as a tribute due to
their fuperior merit, and a teftimony of the
profound refpect, with which he is their

Moft obedient,

Humble Servant,

The AUTHOR.

EDGE-HILL:

A

POEM.

In FOUR BOOKS.

THE SECOND EDITION, CORRECTED AND ENLARGED.

" Salve, magna parens frugum, Saturnia tellus,
" Magna virum! tibi res antiquæ laudis, et artes
" Ingredior, fanctos aufus recludere fontes."

                                        VIRG.

"Our Sight is the moſt perfect, and moſt delightful of
"all our ſenſes. It fills the mind with the largeſt variety
"of ideas, converſes with its objects at the greateſt diſtance,
"and continues the longeſt in action without being tired,
"or ſatiated with its proper enjoyment."

SPECT. N° 411, On the Plea-
ſures of Imagination.

PREFACE.

THE following Poem takes its name from a ridge of hills, which is the boundary between the counties of Oxford and Warwick, and remarkable for its beautiful and extenfive profpect, of which the latter forms a confiderable part. This circumftance afforded the writer an opportunity, very agreeable to him, of paying a tribute to his native country, by exhibiting its beauties to the public in a poetical delineation; divided, by an imaginary line, into a number of diftinct fcenes, correfponding with the different times of the day, each forming an entire picture, and containing its due proportion of objects and colouring.

In

In the execution of this defign, he endea-
voured to make it as extenfively interefting
as he could, by the frequent introduction of
general reflections, hiftorical, philofophical,
and moral; and to enliven the defcription by
digreffiohs and epifodes, naturally arifing
from the fubject.

EDGE-

E D G E - H I L L.

B O O K I.

M O R N I N G.

ARGUMENT TO BOOK THE FIRST.

The Subject propos'd. Address. Ascent to the Hill. General View. Comparison. Philosophical Account of the Origin and Formation of Mountains, &c. Morning View, comprehending the South-West Part of the Scene, interspers'd with Elements and Examples of rural Taste; shewing, at the same Time, its Connexion with, and Dependance upon Civil Government; and concluding with an Historical Episode of the Red-Horse.

E D G E - H I L L.

B O O K I.

M O R N I N G.

BRITANNIA's rural charms, and tranquil fcenes,
   Far from the circling ocean, where her fleets,
Like * Eden's nightly guards, majeftic ride,
I fing; O may the theme and kindred foil
Propitious prove, and to th' appointed hill
Invite the Mufes from their cloifter'd fhades,
With me to rove, and harmonize the ftrain!

* MILTON. Paradife Loft, Book iv.

Nor

Nor shall they, for a time, regret the loss

Of their lov'd ISIS, and fair CHERWEL's stream,

While to the north of their own beauteous fields

The pictur'd scene they view, where AVON shapes

His winding way, enlarging as it flows,

Nor hastes to join SABRINA's prouder wave.

Like a tall rampart! here the mountain rears

Its verdant edge; and, if the tuneful Maids

Their presence deign, shall with PARNASSUS vie.

Level, and smooth the track, which thither leads!

Of champaign bold and fair! Its adverse side

Abrupt, and steep! Thanks, MILLER *! to thy paths,

That ease our winding steps! Thanks to the fount,

The trees, the flow'rs, imparting to the sense

Fragrance or dulcet found of murm'ring rill,

And stilling ev'ry tumult in the breast!

And oft the stately tow'rs, that overtop

The rising wood, and oft the broken arch,

Or mould'ring wall, well taught to counterfeit

The waste of time, to solemn thought excite,

And crown with graceful pomp the shaggy hill.

* SANDERSON MILLER, Esquire, of Radway.

So

 * So Virtue paints the steep ascent to fame :
So her aerial residence displays.

  Still let thy friendship, which prepar'd the way,
Attend, and guide me, as my ravish'd sight
O'er the bleak hill, or shelter'd valley roves.
Teach me with just observance to remark
Their various charms, their storied fame record,
And to the visual join the mental search.

  The summit's gain'd! and, from its airy height,
The late-trod plain looks like an inland sea,
View'd from some promontory's hoary head,
With distant shores environ'd; not with face
Glassy, and uniform, but when its waves
Are gently ruffled by the southern gale,
And the tall masts like waving forests rise.

  Such is the scene! that, from the terrac'd hill,
Displays its graces; intermixture sweet
Of lawns and groves, of open and retir'd.
Vales, farms, towns, villas, castles, distant spires,
And hills on hills, with ambient clouds enrob'd,

---

 * See Lord SHAFTSBURY's Judgment of Hercules,

In long fucceffion court the lab'ring fight,

Loft in the bright confufion.   Thus the youth,

Efcap'd from painful drudgery of words,

Views the fair fields of fcience wide difplay'd;

Where PHOEBUS dwells, and all the tuneful Nine;

Perplext awhile he ftands, and now to this,

Now that bleft feat of harmony divine

Explores his way, with giddy rapture tir'd:

Till fome fage MENTOR, whofe experienc'd feet

Have trod the mazy path, directs his fearch,

And leads him wond'ring to their bright abodes.

Come then, my Friend! guide thou th' advent'rous
  Mufe,

And, with thy counfel, regulate her flight.

 Yet, ere the fweet excurfion fhe begins,

O! liften, while, from facred records drawn,

My daring fong unfolds the caufe, whence rofe

This various face of things—of high, and low—

Of rough, and fmooth.   For with its parent earth

Coeval not prevail'd what now appears

Of hill and dale; nor was its new-form'd fhape,

Like a fmooth, polifh'd orb, a furface plain,

       Wanting

Wanting the fweet variety of change,

Concave, convex, the deep, and the fublime :

Nor, from old Ocean's watry bed, were fcoop'd

Its neighb'ring fhores; nor were they now deprefs'd,

Now rais'd by fudden fhocks ; but fafhion'd all

In perfect harmony, by * laws divine,

On paffive matter, at its birth imprefs'd.

WHEN now two days, as mortals count their

    time,

Th' ALMIGHTY had employ'd on man's abode ;

To motion rous'd the dead, inactive mafs,

The dark illumin'd, and the parts terrene

Impelling each to each, the circle form'd,

* Amongft the many fanciful conceits of writers on the fubject, a learned Divine, in his Confutation of Dr. BURNETT's
Theory, fuppofes that hills and mountains might be occa-.
fioned by fermentation, after the manner of leaven in dough;
while others have attributed their production to the feveral
different caufes mentioned above.

    The following folution, by the defcent of water from the
furface of the earth to the center, feem'd moft eafy, and
natural to the author, and is therefore adopted. Vid. WAR-
REN's Geologiæ, 1698.

Compact,

Compact, and firm, of earth's stupendous orb,

With boundless seas, as with a garment cloath'd,

On the third morn he bade the waters flow

Down to their place, and let dry land appear ;

And it was so.   Strait to their deftin'd bed,

From every part, th' obedient waters ran,

Shaping their downward courfe, and, as they found

Resistance varying with the varying foil,

In their retreat they form'd the gentle flope,

Or headlong precipice, or deep-worn dale,

Or valley, ftretching far its winding maze,

As farther ftill their humid train they led,

By Heav'n directed to the * realms below.

   Now firft was feen the variegated face

Of earth's fair orb fhap'd by the plaftic flood :

Now fmooth and level like its liquid plains,

Now, like its ruffled waves, fweet interchange

Of hill and dale, and now a rougher fcene,

Mountains on mountains lifted to the fky.

   * Called in fcripture, the deep, the great deep, the deep
that lieth under, or beneath the earth—the Tartarus or Ere-
bus of the Heathens,

                                   · Such

Such was her infant form, yet unadorn'd!

And in the naked foil the fubtle * ftream

Fretted its winding track. So He ordain'd!

Who form'd the fluid mafs of atoms fmall,

The principles of things! who moift from dry,

From heavy feyer'd light, compacting clofe

The folid glebe, ftratum of rock, or ore,

Or crumbly marl, or clofe tenacious clay,

Or what befide, in wond'rous order rang'd,

Orb within orb, earth's fecret depths contains.

So was the fhapely fphere, on ev'ry fide,

With equal preffure of furrounding air

Suftain'd, of fea and land harmonious form'd.

Nor beauteous cov'ring was withheld, for ftrait,

At the divine command, the verd'rous grafs

Upfprang unfown, with ev'ry feedful herb,

---

* —————————So the watry throng
With ferpent error wand'ring found their way,
And on the wafhy ooze deep channels wore.
Eafy! ere God had bid the ground be dry,
All but within thofe banks, where rivers now
Stream, and perpetual draw their humid train.
                    MILTON. Paradife Loft, Book vii.

Fruit,

Fruit, plant, or tree, pregnant with future ſtore;

God ſaw the whole—And lo! 'twas very good.

But man, ungrateful man! to deadly ill

Soon turn'd the good beſtow'd, with horrid crimes

Polluting earth's fair ſeat, his Maker's gift!

Till mercy cou'd no more with juſtice ſtrive.

   Then wrath divine unbarr'd Heav'n's watry gates,

And loos'd the fountains of the great abyſs.

Again the waters o'er the earth prevail'd.

Hills rear'd their heads in vain.   Full forty days

The flood increas'd, nor, till ſev'n moons had wan'd,

Appear'd the mountain-tops.   Periſh'd all fleſh,

One family except! and all the works

Of Art were ſwept into th' oblivious pool.

In that dread time what change th' avenging flood

Might cauſe in earth's devoted fabric, who

Of mortal birth can tell? Whether again

'Twas to its firſt chaotic * maſs reduc'd,

To be reform'd anew? or, in its orb,

What violence, what † diſruptions it endur'd?

* According to Mr. HUTCHINSON and his followers.
† According to Dr. BURNETT's Theory.

What

What ancient mountains ftood the furious fhock?

What new arofe?   For doubtlefs new there are,

If all are not; ftrong proof exhibiting

Of later rife, and their once fluid ftate,

By ftranger-foffils, in their inmoft bed

Of loofer mould, or marble rock entomb'd,

Or fhell marine, incorp'rate with themfelves:

Nor lefs the * conic hill, with ample bafe,

Or fcarry * flope by rufhing billows torn,

Or * fiffure deep, in the late delug'd foil

Cleft by fucceeding drought, fide anfwering fide,

And curve to adverfe curve exact oppos'd,

Confefs the watry pow'r; while fcatter'd trains,   .

Or rocky fragments, wafh'd from broken hills,

Take up the tale, and fpread it round the globe.

Then, as the flood retir'd, another face

Of things appear'd, another, and the fame!

---

* There are fome remarkable traces of the great event hère treated of, in each of thefe kinds, at Welcombe, near Stratford upon Avon, formerly a feat of the COMBE family, the whole fcene bearing the ftrongeft marks of fome violent conflict of Nature, and particularly of the agency of water.

Taurus,

Taurus, and Libanus, and Atlas feign'd

To prop the skies! and that fam'd Alpine ridge,

Or Appenine, or snow-clad Caucasus,

Or Ararat on whose emergent top

First moor'd that precious barque, whose chosen crew

Again o'erspread earth's universal orb.

For now, as at the first, from ev'ry side

Hasted the waters to their ancient bounds,

The vast abyss! perhaps from thence ascend,

Urg'd by th' incumbent air, thro' mazy clefts

Beneath the deep, or rise in vapours warm,

Piercing the vaulted earth, anon condens'd

Within the lofty mountains' secret cells,

Ere they their summit gain, down their steep sides

To trickle in a never-ceasing * round.

So

* May not the ebbing and flowing of the sea, to whatever
cause it is owing, tend to assist this operation, as the pulsa-
tion of the heart accelerates the circulation of the blood in
animal bodies?

The reader may see this hypothesis very ably supported by
Mr. CATCOT, in his Essay on the Deluge, 2d edit. together with many respectable names, ancient and modern,
by whom it is patronized. The following passage from
LUCRETIUS

So up the porous ftone, or cryftal tube
The philofophic eye with wonder views
The tinctur'd fluid rife ; fo tepid dews
From chymic founts in copious ftreams diftil.

Such is the ftructure, fuch the wave-worn face
Of Earth's huge fabric! beauteous to the fight,
* And ftor'd with wonders, to th' attentive mind
Confirming, with perfuafive eloquence
Drawn from the rocky mount, or watry fen,
Thofe facred pages, which record the paft,
And awfully predict its future doom.

LUCRETIUS is quoted by him, as well expreffing their
general meaning.
    Partim quod fubter per terras diditur omnes.
    Percolatur enim virus, retroque remanat
    Materies humoris, et ad caput amnibus omnis
    Convenit, unde fuper terras fluit agmine dulci,
    Quà via fecta femel liquido pede detulit undas.

* Trees of a very large fize, torn up by the roots, and other
vegetable and animal bodies, the fpoils of the deluge, are
found in every part of the earth, but chiefly in fens, or
bogs, or amongft peat-earth, which is an affemblage of de-
cayed vegetables.
        See WOODWARD's Nat. Hift. of the Earth, &c.

Now, while the fun its heav'nly radiance fheds

Acrofs the vale, difclofing all its charms,

Emblem of that fair Light, at whofe approach

The Gentile darknefs fled ! ye nymphs, and fwains !

Come hafte with me, while now 'tis early morn,

Thro' UPTON's * airy fields, to where yon' point

Projecting hides NORTHAMPTON's ancient feat †

Retir'd, and hid amidft furrounding fhades :

Counting a length of honourable years,

And folid worth ; while painted BELVIDERES,

Naked, aloft, and built but to be feen,

Shrink at the fun, and totter to the wind.

So fober Senfe oft fhuns the public view,

In privacy conceal'd, while the pert fons

Of Folly flutter in the glare of day.

Hence, o'er the plain, where ftrip'd with alleys
        green,

The golden harveft nods, let me your view

---

* UPTON, the feat of ROBERT CHILD, Efq.

† COMPTON-WINYATE, a feat of the Right Hon. the
Earl of NORTHAMPTON, at the foot of EDGE-HILL.

Progreffive

Progreffive lead to * VERNEY's fifter walls,

Alike in honour, as in name allied !

Alike her walls a noble mafter own,

Studious of elegance.   At his command,

New pillars grace the dome with Grecian pomp

Of Corinth's gay defign.   At his command,

On hill, or plain, new culture cloaths the fcene

With verdant grafs, or variegated grove ;

And bubbling rills in fweeter notes difcharge

Their liquid ftores.   Along the winding vale,

At his command, obfervant of the fhore,

The glitt'ring ftream, with correfpondent grace,

Its courfe purfues, and o'er th' exulting wave

The ftately bridge a beauteous form difplays.

On either fide, rich as th' embroider'd floor

From Perfia's gaudy looms, and firm as fair,

The chequer'd lawns with count'nance blithe proclaim

The Graces reign.   Plains, hills, and woods reply

The Graces reign, and Nature fmiles applaufe.

Smile on, fair fource of beauty, fource of blifs !

* COMPTON-VERNEY, a feat of the Right Hon. Lord
WILLOUGHBY DE BROKE.

To crown the mafter's coft, and deck her path

Who fhares his joy, of gentleft manners join'd

With manly fenfe, train'd to the love refin'd

Of Nature's charms in * WROXTON's beauteous groves.

    Thy neighb'ring villa's ever open gate,

And feftive board, O † WALTON! next invite

The pleafing toil.   Unwilling who can pay

To thee the votive ftrain? For Science here,

And Candour dwell, prepar'd alike to chear

The ftranger-gueft, or for the nation's weal

To pour the ftores mature of wifdom forth,

In fenatorial councils often prov'd,

And, by the public voice attefted long,

Long may it be! with well-deferv'd applaufe.

And fee, beneath the fhade of full-grown elm,

Or near the border of the winding brook,

Skirting the graffy lawn, her polifh'd train

Walks forth to tafte the fragrance of the grove,

---

    * WROXTON, the feat of the Right Hon. the Earl of GUILFORD, father of Lady WILLOUGHBY DE BROKE.

    † WALTON, the feat of Sir CHARLES MORDAUNT, Bart. many years a Member of Parliament for the county of WARWICK.

Woodbine,

Woodbine, or rofe, or to the upland fcene
Of wildly-planted hill, or trickling ftream
From the pure rock, or mofs-lin'd grottos cool,
The Naiads' humid cell! protract the way
With learned converfe, or ingenuous fong.
The fearch purfue to * CHARLECOTE's fair domain,
Where Avon's fportive ftream delighted ftrays
Thro' the gay fmiling meads, and to his bed,
HELE's gentle current wooes, by LUCY's hand
In ev'ry graceful ornament attir'd,
And worthier, fuch, to fhare his liquid realms !

   Near, nor unmindful of th' increafing flood,
STRATFORD her fpacious magazines unfolds,
And hails th' unwieldly barge from weftern fhores,
With foreign dainties fraught, or native ore
Of pitchy hue, to pile the fewell'd grate
In woolly ftores, or hufky grain repay'd.
To fpeed her wealth, lo ! the proud Bridge † extends

  * CHARLECOTE, the feat of GEORGE LUCY, Efq.
  † This Bridge was built in the reign of K. HENRY VII.
at the fole coft and charge of Sir HUGH CLOPTON, Knt.
Lord Mayor of the City of LONDON, and a native of this
place.

           His

His num'rous arches, ftately monument

Of old munificence, and pious love

Of native foil! There STOWER exulting pays

His tributary ftream, well pleas'd with wave

Auxiliary her pond'rous ftores to waft;

And boafting, as he flows, of growing fame,

And wond'rous beauties on his banks difplay'd—

Of ALSCOT's * fwelling lawns, and fretted fpires

Of faireft model, Gothic, or Chinefe—

Of EATINGTON's †, and TOLTON's ‡ verdant meads,

And groves of various leaf, and HONINGTON ‖,

Profufe of charms, and Attic elegance;

Nor fails he to relate, in jocund mood,

How liberally the mafters of the fcene

Enlarge his current, and direct his courfe

With winding grace—and how his cryftal wave

* The feat of JAMES WEST, Efq.

† The feat of the Hon. GEORGE SHIRLEY, Efq.

‡ The feat of Sir HENRY PARKER, Bart.

‖ The feat of JOSEPH TOWNSHEND, Efq.

Reflects

Reflects th' inverted fpires, and pillar'd domes—
And how the frifking deer play on his fides,
Pict'ring their branched heads, with wanton fport,
In his clear face. ̀ Pleas'd with the vaunting tale,
Nor jealous of his fame, Avon receives
The prattling ftream, and, towards thy nobler flood,
Sabrina fair, purfues his length'ning way.

　　Hail, beauteous Avon, hail! on whofe fair banks
The fmiling daifies, and their fifter tribes,
Violets, and cuckow-buds, and lady-fmocks,
A brighter dye difclofe, and proudly tell
That Shakespeare, as he ftray'd thefe meads along,
Their fimple charms admir'd, and in his verfe
Preferv'd, in never-fading bloom to live.

　　And thou, whofe birth thefe walls unrival'd boaft,
That mock'ft the rules of the proud Stagyrite,
And Learning's tedious toil, hail mighty Bard!
Thou great Magician hail! Thy piercing thought
Unaided faw each movement of the mind,
As fkilful artifts view the fmall machine,
The fecret fprings and nice dependencies,

And to thy mimic scenes, by fancy wrought
To such a wond'rous shape, th' impassion'd breast
In floods of grief, or peals of laughter bow'd,
Obedient to the wonder-working strain,
Like the tun'd string responsive to the touch,
Or to the wizard's charm, the passive storm.
Humour and wit, the tragic pomp, or phrase
Familiar flow'd, spontaneous from thy tongue,
As flowers from Nature's lap.—Thy potent spells
From their bright seats aerial sprites detain'd,
Or from their unseen haunts, and slumb'ring shades
Awak'd the fairy tribes, with jocund step
The circled green, and leafy hall to tread:
While, from his dripping caves, old Avon sent
His willing Naiads to their harmless rout.

   Alas! how languid is the labour'd song,
The slow result of rules, and tortur'd sense,
Compar'd with thine! thy animated thought,
And glowing phrase! which art in vain essays,
And schools can never teach. Yet, though deny'd
Thy pow'rs, by situation more allied,

I court

I court the genius of thy fportive Mufe
On Avon's bank, her facred haunts explore,
And hear in ev'ry breeze her charming notes.

    Beyond thefe flow'ry meads, with claffic ftreams
Enrich'd, two fifter rills their currents join,
And Ikenild difplays his Roman pride.
There Alcester * her ancient honour boafts.
But fairer fame, and far more happy lot
She boafts, O Ragley †! in thy courtly train
Of Hertford's fplendid line! Lo! from thefe
       fhades,
Ev'n now his fov'reign, ftudious of her weal,
Calls him to bear his delegated rule
To Britain's fifter ifle. Hibernia's fons
Applaud the choice, and hail him to their fhore
With cordial gratulation. Him, well-pleas'd
With more than filial rev'rence to obey,
Beauchamp attends. What fon, but wou'd rejoice

    * So called from its fituation on the river Alenus, or
Alne, and from its being a *Roman* ftation on the Ikenild-
Street.

    † A feat of the Right Hon. the Earl of Hertford.

                     The

The deeds of such a father to record !

What father, but were bleft in such a son !

Nor may the Muse omit with Conway's * name

To grace her song.   O ! might it worthy flow

Of thofe her theme involves ! The cyder-land,

In Georgic ftrains, by her own Philips fung,

Shou'd boaft no brighter fame, though proudly grac'd

With loftieft-titled names—The Cecil line,

Or Beaufort's, or, O Chandois ! thine, or his

In Anna's councils high, her fav'rite peer,

Harley ! by me ftill honour'd in his race.

See, how the pillar'd ifles and ftately dome

Brighten the woodland-fhade ! while fcatter'd hills,

Airy, and light, in many a conic form,

A theatre compofe, grotefque and wild,

And, with their fhaggy fides, contract the vale

Winding, in ftraiten'd circuit, round their bafe.

Beneath their waving umbrage Flora fpreads

Her fpotted couch, primrofe, and hyacinth

* The Right Hon. Henry Seymour Conway, Efq;
one of his Majefty's principal Secretaries of State, and
brother to the Right Hon. the Earl of Hertford.

                                        Profufe,

Profufe, with ev'ry fimpler bud that blows

On hill or dale.   Such too thy flow'ry pride

O Hewel * ! by thy mafter's lib'ral hand

Advanc'd to rural fame! Such Umberslade † !

In the fweet labour join'd, with culture fair,

And fplendid arts, from Arden's ‡ woodland fhades

The pois'nous damps, and favage gloom to chafe.

What happy lot attends your calm retreats,

By no fcant bound'ry, nor obftructing fence,

Immur'd, or circumfcrib'd ; but fpread at large

In open day : fave what to cool recefs

Is deftin'd voluntary, not conftrain'd

By fad neceffity, and cafual ftate

Of fickly peace ! Such as the moated hall,

With clofe circumference of watry guard,

And penfile bridge proclaim ! or, rear'd aloft,

And inacceffible the maffy tow'rs,

And narrow circuit of embattled walls,

* The feat of the Right Hon. the Earl of Plymouth.

† The feat of the Right Hon. Lord Archer.

‡ The foreft, or woodland part of Warwickshire.

Rais'd

Rais'd on the mountain-precipice! Such thine

O BEAUDESERT *! old MONTFORT's lofty feat!

Haunt of my youthful fteps! where I was wont

To range, chaunting my rude notes to the wind,

While SOMERVILLE difdain'd not to regard

With candid ear, and regulate the ftrain.

Such was the genius of the Gothic age,

And NORMAN policy! Such the retreats

Of BRITAIN's ancient Nobles! lefs intent

On rural beauty, and fweet patronage

Of gentle arts, than ftudious to reftrain,

With fervile awe, Barbarian multitudes;

Or, with confed'rate force, the regal pow'r

Controul. Hence proudly they their vaffal troops

Affembling, now the fate of empire plann'd:

Now o'er defencelefs tribes, with wanton rage,

Tyrannic rul'd; and, in their caftled halls

Secure, with wild excefs their revels kept,

While many a fturdy youth, or beauteous maid,

Sole folace of their parents' drooping age!

* So called, from its pleafant rural fituation.

Bewail'd

Bewail'd their wretched fate, by force compell'd
To thefe abhorr'd abodes! Hence frequent * wars,
In ancient annals fam'd! Hence haply feign'd
Th' enchanted caftle, and its curfed train
Of giants, fpectres, and magicians dire!
Hence gen'rous minds, with indignation fir'd,
And threat'ning fierce revenge, were character'd
By gallant knights on bold atchievements bent,
Subduing monfters, and diffolving fpells.

Thus, from the rural landfcape, learn to know
The various characters of ·time and place.
To hail, from open fcenes, and cultur'd fields,
Fair Liberty, and Freedom's gen'rous reign,
With guardian laws, and polifh'd arts adorn'd.
While the portcullis huge, or moated fence
The fad reverfe of favage times betray—
Diftruft, barbarity, and Gothic rule.

Wou'd ye, with faultlefs judgment, learn to plan
The rural feat? To copy, as ye rove,
The well-form'd picture, and correct defign?
Firft fhun the falfe extremes of high, and low.

* Called the Barons wars.

With

With watry vapours this your fretted walls

Will foon deface; and that, with rough affault,

And frequent tempefts fhake your tott'ring roof.

Me moft the gentle eminence delights

Of healthy champaign, to the funny fouth

Fair-op'ning, and with woods, and circling hills,

Nor too remote, nor, with too clofe embrace,

Stopping the buxom air, behind enclos'd.

But if your lot hath fall'n in fields lefs fair,

Confult their genius, and, with due regard

To Nature's clear directions, fhape your plan.

The fite too lofty fhelter, and the low

With funny lawns, and open areas chear.

The marifh drain, and, with capacious urns,

And well-conducted ftreams refrefh the dry.

So fhall your lawns with healthful verdure fmile,

While others, fick'ning at the fultry blaze,

A ruffet wild difplay, or the rank blade,

And matted tufts the carelefs owner fhame.

Seek not, with fruitlefs coft, the level plain

To raife aloft, nor fink the rifing hill.

Each has its charms tho' diff'rent, each in kind

Improve,

Improve, not alter.   Art with art conceal.

Let no ftrait terrac'd lines your flopes deform.

No barb'rous walls reftrain the bounded fight.

But to the diftant fields the clofer fcene

Connect.   The fpacious lawn with fcatter'd trees

Irregular, in beauteous negligence,

Clothe bountiful.   Your unimprifon'd eye,

With pleafing freedom, thro' the lofty maze

Shall rove, and find no dull fatiety.

The fportive ftream with ftiffen'd line avoid

To torture, nor prefer the long canal,

Or labour'd fount to Nature's eafy flow.

Your winding paths, now to the funny * gleam

Directed, now with high embow'ring trees,

Or fragrant fhrubs conceal'd, with frequent feat,

And rural ftructure deck.   Their pleafing form

To fancy's eye fuggefts inhabitants

Of more than mortal make, and their cool fhade,

And friendly fhelter to refrefhment fweet,

And wholefome meditation fhall invite.

* Hæc amat obfcurum, volet hæc fub luce videri.

HOR.

10   To

To ev'ry ſtructure give its proper ſite.

Nor, on the dreary heath, the gay alcove,

Nor the lone hermit's cell, or mournful urn

Build on the ſprightly lawn. The graſſy ſlope

And ſhelter'd border for the cool arcade

Or Tuſcan porch reſerve. To the chaſte dome,

And fair rotunda give the ſwelling mount

Of freſheſt green. If to the Gothic ſcene

Your taſte incline, in the well-water'd vale,

With lofty pines embrown'd, the mimic fane,

And mould'ring abbey's fretted windows place.

The craggy rock, or precipitious hill,

Shall well become the caſtle's maſſy walls.

In royal villas the Palladian arch,

And Grecian portico, with dignity,

Their pride diſplay : ill ſuits their lofty rank

The ſimpler ſcene. If chance hiſtoric deeds

Your fields diſtinguiſh, count them doubly fair,

And ſtudious aid, with monumental ſtone,

And faithful comment, fancy's fond review.

Now other hills, with other wonders ſtor'd,

Invite the ſearch. In vain ! unleſs the Muſe

The

The landfcape order.   Nor will fhe decline

The pleafing tafk.   For not to her 'tis hard

To foar above the mountain's airy height,

With tow'ring pinions, or, with gentler wing,

T' explore the cool recefles of the vale.

Her piercing eye extends beyond the reach

Of optic tube, levell'd by midnight fage,

At the moon's difk, or other diftant fun,

And planetary worlds beyond the orb

Of Saturn.   Nor can intervening rocks

Impede her fearch.   Alike the fylvan gloom,

Or earth's profoundeft caverns fhe pervades,

And, to her fav'rite fons, makes vifible

All that may grace, or dignify the fong,

Howe'er envelop'd from their mortal ken.

  So Uriel, winged regent of the fun!

Upon its evening-beam to Paradife

Came gliding down; fo, on its floping ray,

To his bright charge return'd.   So *th' heav'nly gueft,*

From Adam's eyes the carnal film remov'd,

On Eden's hill, and purg'd his vifual nerve

To fee things yet unform'd, and future deeds.

                    D   Lo!

Lo! where the fouthern hill, with winding courfe,

Bends tow'rd the weft, and, from his airy feat,

Views four fair provinces in union join'd;

Beneath his feet, confpicuous rais'd, and rude,

A maffy pillar rears its fhapelefs head.

Others in ftature lefs, an area fmooth

Inclofe, like that on * Sarum's ancient plain.

And fome of middle rank apart are feen:

Diftinguifh'd thofe! by courtly character

Of knights, while that the regal † title bears.

What now the circle drear, and ftiffen'd mafs

Compofe, like us, were animated forms,

With vital warmth, and fenfe, and thought endued;

A band of warriors brave! Effect accurs'd

Of necromantic art, and fpells impure.

So vulgar fame. But clerks, in antique lore

Profoundly fkill'd, far other ftory tell:

And, in its myftic form, temple, or court

Efpy, to fabled gods, or throned kings

* Stone-henge.

† Call'd the King's-stone, or Koning-stone.

Devote;

Devote; or fabric monumental, rais'd

By Saxon hands, or by that Danish chief

ROLLO * ! the builder in the name imply'd.

   Yet to the west the pleasing search pursue,

Where from the vale, BRAILS lifts his scarry sides,

And ILLMINGTON, and CAMPDEN's hoary hills,

(By LYTTELTON's sweet plaint, and thy abode

His matchless LUCIA ! to the Muse endear'd)

Impress new grandeur on the spreading scene,

With champaign fields, broad plain, and covert vale

Diversified: By CERES some adorn'd

With rich luxuriance of golden grain,

And some in FLORA's liv'ry gaily dight,

And some with sylvan honours graceful crown'd.

Witness the forest-glades, with stately pride,

Surrounding SHELDON's † venerable dome!

Witness the sloping lawns of IDLICOT ‡ !

---

* Call'd ROLL-RICH-STONES.

† WESTON, the seat of WILLIAM SHELDON, Esq.

‡ The seat of the late Baron LEGGE, now belonging to ROBERT LADBROKE, Esq.

And

And Honington's irriguous meads! Some wind
Meand'ring round the hills disjoin'd, remote,
Giving full licenfe to their fportive range;
While diftant, but diftinct, his Alpine ridge
Malvern erects o'er Esham's vale fublime,
And boldly terminates the finifh'd fcene.

Still are the praifes of the Red-Horse Vale
Unfung; as oft it happens to the mind
Intent on diftant themes, while what's more near,
And nearer, more important, 'fcapes its note.

From yonder far-known hill, where the thin turf
But ill conceals the ruddy glebe, a form
On the bare foil portray'd, like that fam'd fteed,
Which, in its womb, the fate of Troy conceal'd,
O'erlooks the vale.—Ye fwains, that wifh to learn,
Whence rofe the ftrange phænomenon, attend!

Britannia's fons, tho' now for arts renown'd,
A race of anceftors untaught, and rude,
Acknowledge; like thofe naked Indian tribes,
Which firft Columbus in the Atlantic ifles
With wonder faw. Alike their early fate,

To

To yield to conquering arms! Imperial ROME
Was then to them what BRITAIN is to thefe,
And thro' the fubject-land her trophies rear'd.

But haughty ROME, her ancient manners flown,
Stoop'd to Barbaric rage.   O'er her proud walls
The Goths prevail, which erft the Punic bands
Affail'd in vain, tho' Cannæ's bloody field
Their valour own'd, and HANNIBAL their guide!
Such is the fate, which mightieft empires prove,
Unlefs the virtues of the fon preferve
What his forefather's ruder courage won!

   * No CATO now, the lift'ning fenate warm'd
To love of virtuous deeds, and public weal.
No SCIPIOS led her hardy fons to war,
With fenfe of glory fir'd.   Thro' all her realms
Or hoftile arms invade, or factions fhake
Her tott'ring ftate.   From her proud capitol

---

   * Non his juventus orta parentibus
     Infecit æquor fanguine Punico,
     Pyrrhumque, et ingentem cecidit
     Antilochum, Hannibalemque dirum.
                              HORAT.

                    D 3   Her

Her tutelary gods retire, and ROME,

Imperial ROME, once miftrefs of the world,

A victim falls, fo righteous Heav'n ordains,

To Pride and Luxury's all-conqu'ring charms.

    Mean time her ancient foes, ere while reftrain'd

By Roman arms, from Caledonia's hills

Rufh like a torrent, with refiftlefs force,

O'er Britain's fencelefs bounds, and thro'. her fields

Pour the full tide of defolating war.

ÆTIUS, thrice Conful! now an empty name,

In vain her fons invoke.   In vain they feek

Relief in fervitude.   Ev'n fervitude

Its miferable comforts now denies,

From fhore to fhore they fly.   The briny flood,

A guardian once, their further flight reftrains.

Some court the boift'rous deep, a milder foe,

Some gain the diftant fhores, and fondly hope

In each to find a more indulgent home.

The reft, protracting ftill a wretched life,

From Belgia's coaft in wild defpair invite

Its new inhabitants, a Saxon race!

On enterprize, and martial conqueft bent.

With

With joy the Saxons to their aid repair,

And foon revenge them on their northern foes.

Revenge too dearly bought! Thefe courted guefts

Give them fhort fpace for joy.   A hoftile look

On their fair fields they caft, (for feeble hands

Alas! too fair,) and feize them for their own.

And now again the conquer'd ifle affumes

Another form; on ev'ry plain, and hill

New marks exhibiting of fervile ftate,

The maffy ftone with figures quaint infcrib'd—

Or dyke by * WODEN, or the Mercian King †,

Vaft bound'ry made—or thine, O ASHBURY ‡ !

And TYSOE's ‖ wond'rous theme, the martial Horfe,

---

* WANSDYKE, or WODENSDYKE, a boundary of the kingdom of the Weft Saxons, in Wiltfhire.

† OFFA, from whom the boundary between the kingdom of the Mercians, and the Britons in WALES, took its name.

‡ ASHBURY, in BERKSHIRE, near which is the figure of a horfe cut on the fide of a hill, in whitifh earth, which gives name to the neighbouring valley.

‖ The figure of the Red Horfe, here defcribed, is in the parifh of TYSOE.

Carv'd

Carv'd on the yielding turf, armorial fign

Of HENGIST, Saxon Chief! of BRUNSWICK now,

And with the Britifh lion join'd, the bird

Of Rome furpaffing. Studious to preferve

The fav'rite form, the treach'rous conquerors

Their vaffal tribes compel, with feftive rites,

Its fading figure yearly to renew,

And to the neighb'ring * vale impart its name.

* Call'd, from this figure, the VALE of RED-HORSE.

END OF THE FIRST BOOK.

EDGE.

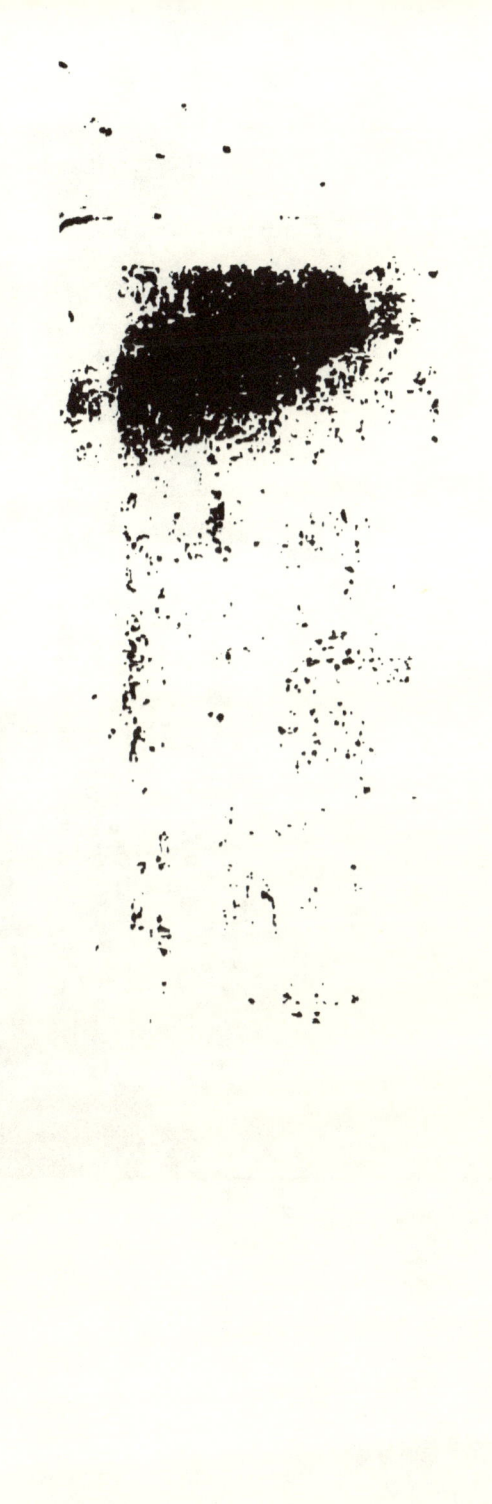

to face page 41.

EDGE-HILL.

BOOK II.

NOON.

ARGUMENT TO BOOK THE SECOND:

Noon. *The Mid-Scene from the Castle on* RATLEY-HILL. *More particular Account of the several Parts of this Scene, and of whatever is most remarkable in it.* WARWICK. *Its Antiquity.* *Historical Account of the Earls of* WARWICK. *Story of* GUY. GUY'S-CLIFFE. KENELWORTH. *Its Castle.* *History of it.* BALSAL. WROXAL. COVENTRY. *Its Environs.* *Manufactures.* *Story of* GODIVA. *Peroration.*

E D G E - H I L L.

B O O K II.

N O O N.

THE Sun, whofe eaftern ray had fcarcely gilt
    The mountain's brow, while up the fteep afcent,
With early ftep, we climb'd, now wide difplays
His radiant orb, and half his daily ftage
Hath nearly meafur'd. From th' illumin'd vale
The foaring mifts are drain'd, and, o'er the hill,
No more breathes grateful the cool, balmy air,
Chearing our fearch, and urging on our fteps
                        Delightful.

Delightful. See, the languid herds forſake

The burning mead, and creep beneath the ſhade

Of ſpreading tree, or ſhelt'ring hedge-row tall:

Or, in the mant'ling pool, rude reſervoir

Of wintry rains, and the ſlow, thrifty ſpring!

Cool their parch'd limbs, and lave their panting ſides,

   Let us too ſeek the ſhade. Yon' airy dome,

Beneath whoſe lofty battlements we found

A covert paſſage to theſe ſultry realms,

Invites our drooping ſtrength, and well befriends

The pleaſing comment on fair Nature's book,

In ſumptuous volume, open'd to our view.

   Ye ſportive nymphs! that o'er the rural ſcene

Preſide, you chief! that haunt the flow'ry banks

Of Avon, where, with more majeſtic wave,

Warwick's illuſtrious Lord, thro' the gay meads

His dancing current guides, or round the lawn

Directs th' embroider'd verge of various dyes,

O! teach me all its graces to unfold,

And, with your praiſe, join his attendant fame.

   'Tis well! Here ſhelter'd from the ſcorching heat,

At large we view the ſubject vale ſublime,

                        And

And unimpeded.   Hence its limits trace

Stretching, in wanton bound'ry, from the foot

Of this green mountain, far as human ken

Can reach, a theatre immenſe! adorn'd

With ornaments of ſweet variety,

By Nature's pencil drawn—the level meads,

A verdant floor! with brighteſt gems inlaid,

And richly-painted flow'rs—the tillag'd plain,

Wide-waving to the ſun a rival blaze

Of gold, beſt ſource of wealth!—the prouder hills,

With outline fair, in naked pomp diſplay'd,

Round, angular, oblong; and others crown'd

With graceful foliage.   Over all her horn

Fair Plenty pours, and Cultivation ſpreads

Her height'ning luſtre.   See, beneath her touch,

The ſmiling harveſts riſe, with bending line,

And wavy ridge, along the dappled glebe

Stretching their lengthen'd beds.   Her careful hand

Piles up the yellow grain, or ruſtling hay

Aduſt for wintry ſtore—the long-ridg'd mow,

Or ſhapely pyramid, with conic roof,

Dreſſing the landſcape.   She the thick-wove fence

Nurſes,

Nurſes, and adds, with care, the hedge-row elm.

Around her farms and villages ſhe plans

The rural garden, yielding wholeſome food

Of ſimple viands, and the fragrant herb

Medicinal.   The well-rang'd orchard now

She orders, or the ſhelt'ring clump, or tuft

Of hardy trees, the wintry ſtorms to curb,

Or guard the ſweet retreat of village-ſwain,

With health, and plenty crown'd. Fair Science next,

Her offspring! adds towns, cities, vaulted domes,

And ſplendid palaces, and chaſes large,

With lake, and planted grove.   Hence WARWICK,
        fair

With riſing buildings, COVENTRY's tall ſpires,

And KENELWORTH! thy ſtately caſtle roſe,

Which ſtill, in ruin, charms th' aſtoniſh'd ſight.

To crown the beauteous ſcene, the curtain'd ſky,

Its canopy divine of azure tint,

Spreads heav'nly fair, and ſoftens ev'ry charm.

   Now yet again, with accurate ſurvey,

The level plain, hills riſing various, woods,

And meadows green, the ſimple cot, and towns,

                                    Nurs'ries

Nurs'ries of arts, and commerce! WARWICK, fair
With rifing buildings, COVENTRY's tall fpires,
Magnificent in ruin KENELWORTH!
And ftill more diftant fcenes, with legends ftrange,
And fmoaky arts, taught in the dufky fchools
Of TUBAL's fons, attentive let us fcan,
And all their charms, and myfteries explore.

 Firft view, but cautious, the vaft precipice;
Left, ftartled at the giddy height, thy fenfe
Swimming forfake thee, and thy trembling limbs,
Unnerv'd, and fault'ring, threaten dang'rous lapfe.
Along th' indented bank, the foreft-tribes,
The thin-leav'd afh, dark oak, and gloffy beech,
Of polifh'd rind, their branching boughs extend,
With blended tints, and amicable ftrife,
Forming a checker'd fhade. Below, the lawns,
With fpacious fweep, and wild declivity,
To yellow plains their floping verdure join.

 There, white with flocks, and, in her num'rous herds
Exulting, CHADSUNT's * paftures, large, and fair

---

 * The feat of JAMES NEWSAM CRAGGS, Efq.

Salute

Salute the fight, and witnefs to the fame

Of LICHFIELD's mitred faint *.   The furzy heaths

Succeed; clofe refuge of the tim'rous Hare,

Or prowling Fox, but refuge infecure!

From their dark covert oft the hunter-train

Roufe them unwilling, and, o'er hill, and dale,

With wild, tumultuous joy, their fteps purfue.

Juft vengeance on the midnight thief! and life

With life aton'd! But that poor, trembling wretch!

' Who doubts if now fhe lives,' what hath fhe done;

Guiltlefs of blood, and impotent of wrong?

How num'rous, how infatiate yet her foes!

Ev'n in thefe thickets, where fhe vainly fought

A fafe retreat from man's unfeeling race,

The bufy hound, to blood, and flaughter train'd,

Snuffs her fweet vapour, and, to murth'rous rage,

By mad'ning founds impell'd, in her clofe feat,

With fury tears her, and her corfe devours:

Or fcares her o'er the fields, and, by the fcent,

With keen defire of reeking gore inflam'd,

* ST. CHADD.

Loud-

Loud-bellowing tortures her with deathful cries.

Nor more fecure her *path!* Man even there,

Watching, with foul intent, her fecret haunts,

Plants inftruments of death, and round her neck

The fatal fnare entwines. Thus Innocence,

In human things, by wily Fraud enfnar'd,

Oft helplefs falls, while the bold Plund'rer 'fcapes.

Next the wide champaign, and the cheerful downs

Claim notice; chiefly thine, O CHESTERTON *!

Pre-eminent. Nor 'fcape the roving eye

Thy folemn wood, and Roman veftiges,

Encampment green, or military road!

Amufive to the grave, hiftoric mind.

Thee † TACHBROKE joins with venerable fhade.

Nor diftant far, in Saxon annals fam'd,

The rural ‡ court of OFFA, Mercian King!

---

* A feat of the Right Honourable Lord WILLOUGHBY DE BROKE, fo called from its being a Roman ftation on the Fofs-Way.

† A feat of Sir WALTER BAGOT, Bart.

‡ OFFCHURCH, the feat of WHITWICK KNIGHTLEY, Efq.

E Where,

Where, fever'd from its trunk, low lies the head

Of brave FERMUNDUS, flain by coward hands,

As on the turf fupine in fleep he lay,

Nor.wift it fleep from which to wake no more!

   Now WARWICK claims the fong; fupremely fair

In this fair realm; confpicuous rais'd to view

On the firm rock, a beauteous eminence

For health, and pleafure form'd.   Full to the fouth

A ftately range of high, embattled walls

And lofty tow'rs, and precipices vaft,

* Its guardian worth, and ancient pomp confefs.

† The northern hills, where Superftition long

Her gloomy rites maintain'd, a tranquil fcene

Of gentler arts, and pleafures more refin'd

Difplays.   Lawns, parks, and meadows fair,

And groves around their mingled graces join,

And AVON pours his tributary ftream.

   ‡ On thee contending kings their bounty pour'd,

And call'd the favour'd city by their names.

                                          Thy

* The Caftle.

† The Priory, now the feat of HENRY WISE, Efq.

‡ Called CAER-LEON from GUTH-LEON, alfo CAER-

   7   GWAYR,

* Thy worth the Romans publiſh'd, when to thee

Their legions they conſign'd.   Thee ETHELFLEDE †,

Thy guardian Fair! with royal grace reſtor'd,

When Pagan foes had raz'd thy goodly ſtreets.

A monarch's care, thoſe walls ‡ to learning rais'd,

§ Theſe an aſylum to declining age

A LEICESTER's love proclaim.   Nor paſs unſung

The train of gallant chiefs, by thy lov'd name

Diſtinguiſh'd, and by deeds of high renown

Gracing the lofty title.   ‖ ARTHGAL firſt,

And brave MORVIDUS, fam'd in Druid ſong,

And Britiſh annals.   Fair FELICIA's ſire,

ROHAND ! and with her join'd in wedded love,

GWAYR, or GUARIC, from GWAR, two Britiſh Kings. Its preſent name is ſaid to be taken from WARREMUND, a Saxon.

  * It was the PRÆSIDIUM of the Romans.

  † She rebuilt it when it had been deſtroyed by the Danes.

  ‡ The Free-School.

  § The Hoſpital.

  ‖ The firſt Earl of WARWICK, and one of the Knights of King ARTHUR's round table.

Immortal

Immortal Guy! who near Wintonia's walls

With that gigantic braggard Colebrand hight!

For a long fummer's day fole fight maintain'd.

But huge gigantic fize, and braggart oaths,

And fword, or maffy club difmay'd thee not.

Thy fkill the ftroke eluded, or thy fhield

Harmlefs receiv'd, while on his batter'd fides

Fell thick thy galling blows, till from his hands

Down dropp'd the pond'rous weapon, and himfelf

Proftrate, to thy keen blade his grizly head

Reluctant yielded. Lamentations loud,

And fhouts victorious, in ftrange concert join'd,

Proclaim the champion's fall. Thee Athelstan

His great deliverer owns, and meditates

With honours fair, and feftive pomp to crown.

But other meed thy thoughtful mind employ'd,

Intent in heav'nly folitude to fpend

The precious eve of life. Yet fhall the Mufe

Thy deed record, and on her patriot lift

Enrol thy name, tho' many a Saxon chief

She leaves unfung. A Norman race fucceeds,

To

To thee, fair town *! by charitable deeds,

And pious gifts endear'd.   The BEAUCHAMPS too

Thou claim'ft, for arms, and courtly manners fam'd!

+ Him chief, whom three imperial HENRYS crown'd

With envied honours.   Mirror fair was he

Of valour, and of knightly feats atchiev'd

In tilt, and tournament.   Thee ‡ NEVIL boafts

For bold exploits renown'd, with civil ftrife

. When BRITAIN's bleeding realm her weaknefs

  mourn'd,

And half her nobles in the conteft flain

Of YORK, and LANCASTER.   He, fworn to both,

As int'reft tempted, or refentment fir'd,

 * HENRY DE Novo BURGO, the firft Norman Earl,
founded the priory at Warwick, and ROGER his fon built
and endowed the church of St. Mary.

 + RICHARD Earl of Warwick, in the reigns of K.
HENRY IV. V. and VI. was Governor of Calais, and Lieu-
tenant General of FRANCE. He founded the Lady's Chapel,
and lies interred there under a very magnificent monument.

 ‡ Called MAKE-KING. He was killed at the battle of
Barnet.

To HENRY now, and now to EDWARD join'd

His pow'rful aid ; now both to empire rais'd,

Now from their fummit pluck'd, till in the ftrife

By EDWARD's conquering arms at length he fell.

Thou, * CLARENCE, next, and next thy haplefs fon,

The laft † PLANTAGENET awhile appears

To dignify the lift ; both facrific'd

To barb'rous policy ! Proud ‡ DUDLEY now

From EDWARD's hand the bright diftinction bore,

But foon to MARY paid his forfeit head,

And in his fate a wretched race involv'd :

Thee chief, thee wept by ev'ry gentle Mufe,

Fair § JANE ! untimely doom'd to bloody death,

* He married the Earl of WARWICK's daughter, and was put to death by his brother, EDWARD IV.

† Beheaded in the Tower by HENRY VII. under a pretence of favouring the efcape of Peter Warbeck.

‡ Made Earl of WARWICK by EDWARD VI. and afterwards Duke of NORTHUMBERLAND.

§ Lady JANE GREY, married to a fon of the Earl of WARWICK.

For

For treafon not thy own.   To * Rich's line
Was then transfer'd th' illuftrious name, to thine
O † Greville ! laft.   Late may it there remain !
With promife fair, as now, (more fair what heart
Parental craves ?) of long, tranfmiffive worth,
Proud Warwick's name, with growing fame to grace,
And crown, with lafting joy, her caftled hill.

Hail, ftately pile ; fit manfion for the great !
Worthy the lofty title ! Worthy him ‡,
To Beauchamp's gallant race allied ! the friend

---

* Robert Lord Rich, created Earl of Warwick by
James I.

† Greville Lord Brook, firft created Earl Brook of
Warwick Caftle, and afterwards Earl of Warwick, by
K. George II.

‡ Sir Fulke Greville, made Baron Brook of Beau-
camp's-court, by James I. had the Caftle of Warwick,
then in a ruinous condition, granted to him ; upon which he
laid out 20,000 l.   He lies buried in a neat octagon building,
on the north fide of the chancel at Warwick, under a fine
marble monument, on which is the following very fignificant,
laconic infcription,

" TROPHOEVM PECCATI !
" Fulke Greville, Servant to Queen Elizabeth, Coun-
" fellor to King James, and Friend to Sir Philip Sidney."

Of gentle SIDNEY! to whofe long defert,

In royal councils prov'd, his fov'reign's gift

Confign'd the lofty ftructure : Worthy he!

The lofty ftructure's fplendor to reftore.

Nor lefs intent who now, by lineal right,

His place fuftains, with reparations bold,

And well-attemper'd dignity to grace

Th' embattled walls. Nor fpares his gen'rous mind

The coft of rural work, plantation large,

Foreft, or fragrant fhrub; or fhelter'd walks,

Or ample, verdant lawns, where the fleek deer

Sport on the brink of AVON's flood, or graze

Beneath the rifing walls; magnificence

With grace uniting, and enlarg'd delight

Of profpect fair, and Nature's fmiling fcenes!

Still is the colouring faint. O! cou'd my verfe,

Like their * LOUISA's pencil'd fhades defcribe

The tow'rs, the woods, the lawns, the winding ftream,

Fair like her form, and like her birth fublime!

* The Right Hon. Lady LOUISA GREVILLE, daughter to
the Right Hon. the Earl of WARWICK.

Not

Not Windsor's royal scenes by Denham sung,

Or that more tuneful bard on Twick'nam's shore

Should boast a loftier strain, but in my verse

Their fame shou'd live, as lives, proportion'd true,

Their beauteous image in her graven lines.

Transporting theme! on which I still cou'd waste

The ling'ring hours, and still protract the song

With new delight; but thy example, Guy!

Calls me from scenes of pomp, and earthly pride,

To muse with thee in thy sequester'd cell *.

Here the calm scene lulls the tumultuous breast

To sweet composure.   Here the gliding stream,

That winds its watry path in many a maze, .

As loth to leave th' enchanted spot, invites

To moralize on fleeting time, and life,

With all its treach'rous sweets, and fading joys,

In emblem shewn, by many a short-liv'd flow'r,

That on its margin smiles, and smiling falls

To join its parent Earth.   Here let me delve,

Near thine, my chamber in the peaceful rock,

* Called Guy's Cliff, the seat of the Right Hon. Lady
Mary Greatheed.

And

And think no more of gilded palaces,

And luxury of fenfe. ' From the till'd glebe,

Or ever-teeming brook, my frugal meal

I'll gain, and flake my thirft at yonder fpring.

Like thee, I'll climb the fteep, and mark the fcene

How fair! how paffing fair! in grateful ftrains

Singing the praifes of creative love.

Like thee, I'll tend the call of mattin bell *

To early orifons, and lateft tune

My evening fong to that more wond'rous love,

Which fav'd us from the grand Apoftate's wiles,

And righteous vengeance of Almighty ire,

Juftly incens'd.   O pow'r of grace divine!

When mercy met with truth, with juftice, peace.

Thou, holy Hermit! in this league fecure,

Did'ft wait Death's vanquifh'd fpectre as a friend,

To change thy mortal coil for heav'nly blifs.

　　Next, KENELWORTH! thy fame invites the fong:

Affemblage fweet of focial, and ferene!

But chiefly two fair ftreets, in adverfe rows,

* Here was anciently an oratory, where tradition fays,
Guy fpent the latter part of his life in devotional exercifes.

Their

Their lengthen'd fronts extend, reflecting each

Beauty on each reciprocal.   Between,

A verdant valley, flop'd from either fide,

Forms the mid-fpace, where gently-gliding flows

A cryftal ftream, beneath the mould'ring bafe

Of an old abbey's venerable walls.

Still further in the vale her caftle lifts

Its ftately tow'rs, and tott'ring battlements,

Dreft with the rampant ivy's uncheck'd growth

Luxuriant.   Here let us paufe awhile,

To read the melancholy tale of pomp

Laid low in duft, and, from hiftoric page,

Compofe its epitaph.   Hail, * Clinton ! hail !

Thy Norman founder ftill yon' neighb'ring † Green,

And maffy walls, with ftile ‡ Imperial grac'd,

Record. 'The § Montforts thee with hardy deeds,

* Geoffry de Clinton, who built both the Caftle, and the adjoining Monaftery, Temp. Hen. I.

† Clinton-Green.

‡ Cæsar's-Tower.

§ The Montforts, Earls of Leicester, of which Simon de Montfort, and his fon Henry, were killed at the battle of Evefham.

And

And memorable fiege by * Henry's arms,

And fenatorial acts, that bear thy name

Diftinguifh.   Thee the bold Lancaftrian † line,

A royal train! from valiant Gaunt deriv'd,

Grace with new luftre; till Eliza's hand

Transferr'd thy walls to Leicester's ‡ favour'd Earl.

He long, beneath thy roof, the maiden Queen,

And all her courtly guefts, with rare device

Of mafk, and emblematic fcenery,

Tritons, and fea-nymphs, and the floating ifle,

Detain'd.   Nor feats of prowefs, jouft, or tilt

Of harnefs'd knights, nor ruftic revelry

Were wanting; nor the dance, and fprightly mirth

Beneath the feftive walls, with regal ftate,

And choiceft lux'ry ferv'd.   But regal ftate,

* Henry III. who befieged this Caftle, and call'd a conven-
tion here, which paffed an act for redeeming forfeited eftates,
called Dictum de Kenelworth.

† From whom a part of this ftructure is called Lancaster's Buildings.

‡ Granted by Queen Elizabeth to Dudley Earl of
Leicester.

And

And fprightly mirth, beneath the feftive roof,

Are now no more.   No more affembled crowds

At the ftern porter's lodge admittance crave.

No more, with plaint, or fuit importunate,

The thronged lobby echoes, nor with ftaff,

Or gaudy badge, the bufy purfuivants

Lead to wifh'd audience.   All, alas ! is gone,

And Silence keeps her melancholy court

Throughout the walls; fave, where, in rooms of ftate,

Kings once repos'd ! chatter the wrangling daws,

Or fcreech-owls hoot along the vaulted ifles.

No more the trumpet calls the martial band,

With fprightly fummons, to the guarded lifts ;

Nor lofty galleries their pride difclofe

Of beauteous nymphs in courtly pomp attir'd,

Watching, with trembling hearts, the doubtful ftrife,

And, with their looks, infpiring wond'rous deeds.

No more the lake difplays its pageant fhows,

And emblematic forms.   Alike the lake,

And all its emblematic forms are flown,

And in their place mute flocks, and heifers graze,

Or buxom damfels ted the new-mown hay.

                                        What

What art thou, Grandeur! with thy flatt'ring train

Of pompous lies, and boaftful promifes?

Where are they now, and what's their mighty fum?

All, all are vanifh'd! like the fleeting forms

Drawn in an evening cloud.   Nought now remains,

Save thefe fad relicks of departed pomp,

Thefe fpoils of time, a monumental pile!

Which to the vain its mournful tale relates,

And warns them not to truft to fleeting dreams.

Thee too, tho' boafting not a royal train,

The Mufe, O * BALSHAL! in her faithful page

Shall celebrate : for long beneath thy roof

A band of warriors bold, of high renown,

To martial deeds, and hazardous emprize

Sworn, for defence of SALEM's facred walls;

From Paynim-foes, and holy pilgrimage.

Now other guefts thou entertain'ft,

A female band, by female charity

---

* Formerly a feat of the Knights Templars, now an Álms-
houfe for poor widows, founded by the Lady KATHARINE
LEVISON, a defcendant of ROBERT DUDLEY, Earl of
LEICESTER.

Suftain'd.

Suftain'd.   Thee, * WROXAL! too, in fame allied,

Seat of the Poet's, and the Mufe's friend!

My verfe fhall fing, with thy long-exil'd Knight;

By LEONARD's pray'rs, from diftant fervitude,

To thefe brown thickets, and his mournful mate,

Invifibly convey'd.   Yet doubted fhe

His fpeech, and alter'd form, and better proof

Impatient urg'd.   (So ITHACA's chafte queen

Her much-wifh'd lord, by twice ten abfent years,

And wife MINERVA's guardian care difguis'd,

Acknowledg'd not: fo, with fufpended faith,

His bridal claim reprefs'd.)   Strait he difplays

Part of the nuptial ring between them fhar'd,

When in the bold crufade his fhield he bore.

The twin memorial of their plighted love

Within her faithful bofom fhe retain'd.

Quick from its fhrine the hallow'd pledge fhe drew,

To match it with its mate, when, ftrange to tell!

No fooner had the feparated curves

---

* The feat of CHRISTOPHER WREN, Efq; once a nun-
nery, dedicated to St. LEONARD.—See DUGDALE's Antiquities.

Approach'd

Approach'd each other, but, with fudden fpring,

They join'd again, and the fmall circle clos'd.

So they, long fever'd, met in clofe embrace.

At length, O Coventry! thy neighb'ring fields,

And fair furrounding villas we attend,

* Allesley, and † Whitley's paftures, ‡ Stivi-

CHALE,

That views with lafting joy thy green domains,

And § Bagington's fair walls, and ‖ Stonely! thine,

And ¶ Coombe's majeftic pile, both boafting once

Monaftic pomp, ftill equal in renown!

And, as their kindred fortunes they compare,

Applauding more the prefent, than the paft.

* The feat of M. Neale, Efq.

† The feat of Ed. Bowater, Efq; now belonging to
Francis Wheeler, Efq.

‡ The feat of Arthur Gregory, Efq; commanding a
pleafant view of Coventry park, &c.

§ The feat of William Bromley, Efq; one of the
Reprefentatives in Parliament for the county of Warwick.

‖ The feat of the Right Hon. Lord Leigh.

¶ The feat of the Right Hon. Lord Craven.

Ev'n

Ev'n now the pencil'd fheets, unroll'd, difplay

More fprightly charms of beauteous lawn, and grove,

And fweetly-wand'ring paths, and ambient ftream,

To chear with lafting flow th' enamell'd fcene,

And themes of fong for future bards prepare.

 Fair City! thus environ'd! and thyfelf

For royal grants, and filken arts renown'd!

To thee the docile youth repair, and learn,

With fidelong glance, and nimble ftroke, to ply

The flitting fhuttle, while their active feet,

In myftic movements, prefs the fubtle ftops

Of the loom's complicated frame, contriv'd,

From the loofe thread, to form, with wond'rous art,

A texture clofe, inwrought with choice device

Of flow'r, or foliage gay, to the rich ftuff,

Or filky web, imparting fairer worth.

Nor fhall the Mufe, in her defcriptive fong,

Neglect from dark oblivion to preferve

Thy mould'ring * Crofs, with ornament profufe

---

* Built by Sir WILLIAM HOLLIES, Lord Mayor of LON-
DON, in the reign of King HENRY VIII.

F   Of

Of pinnacles, and niches, proudly rais'd,

Height above height, a fculptur'd chronicle!

Lefs lafting than the monumental verfe.

Nor fcornful will fhe flout thy cavalcade,

Made yearly to Godiva's deathlefs praife,

While gaping crowds around her pageant throng,

With prying look, and ftupid wonderment.

Not fo the Mufe! who, with her virtue fir'd,

And love of thy renown, in notes as chafte

As her fair purpofe, from memorials dark,

Shall, to the lift'ning ear, her tale explain.

When * Edward, laft of Egbert's royal race,

O'er fev'n united realms the fceptre fway'd,

Proud Leofric, with truft of fov'reign pow'r,

The fubject Mercians rul'd.   His lofty ftate

The lovelieft of her fex! a noble dame

Of Thorold's ancient line, Godiva fhar'd.

But pageant pomp charm'd not her faintly mind

Like virtuous deeds, and care of others weal,

Such tender paffions in his haughty breaft

* Edward the Confessor.

He cherifh'd not, but with defpotic fway,

Controul'd his vaffal tribes, and, from their toil,

His luxury maintain'd. Godiva faw

Their plaintive looks ; with grief fhe faw thy fons,

O Coventry ! by tyrant laws opprefs'd,

And urg'd her haughty lord, but urg'd in vain !

With patriot-rule, thy drooping arts to chear.

Yet, tho' forbidden e'er again to move

In what fo much his lofty ftate concern'd,

Not fo from thought of charitable deed

Defifted fhe, but amiably perverfe

Her hopelefs fuit renew'd.   Bold was th' attempt !

Yet not more bold than fair, if pitying fighs

Be fair, and charity which knows no bounds.

What had'ft thou then to fear from wrath inflam'd

At fuch tranfcendent guilt, rebellion join'd

With female weaknefs, and officious zeal ?

So thy ftern lord might call the gen'rous deed ;

Perhaps might punifh as befitted deed

So call'd, if love reftrain'd not : yet tho' love

O'er anger triumph'd, and imperious rule,

Not o'er his pride; which better to maintain,
His anfwer thus he artfully return'd.

   Why will the lovely partner of my joys,
Forbidden, thus her wild petition urge?
Think not my breaft is fteel'd againft the claims
Of fweet humanity.   Think not I hear
Regardlefs thy requeft.   If piety,
Or other motive, with miftaken zeal,
Call'd to thy aid, pierc'd not my ftubborn frame,
Yet to the pleader's worth, and modeft charms,
Wou'd my fond love no trivial gift impart.
But pomp and fame forbid. That vaffalage,
Which, thoughtlefs, thou wou'dft tempt me to diffolve,
Exalts our fplendor, and augments my pow'r.
With tender bofoms form'd, and yielding hearts,
Your fex foon melts at fights of vulgar woe;
Heedlefs how *glory* fires the *manly* breaft
With love of rank fublime.   This principle
In female minds a feebler empire holds,
Oppofing lefs the fpecious arguments
For milder rule, and freedom's popular theme.

                                                   But

But plant fome gentler paffion in its room,

Some virtuous inftinct fuited to your make,

As glory is to ours, alike requir'd

A ranfom for the vulgar's vaffal ftate,

Then wou'dft thou foon the ftrong contention own,

And juftify my conduct.   Thou art fair,

And chafte as fair ; with niceft fenfe of fhame,

And fanctity of thought.   Thy bofom thou

Did'ft ne'er expofe to fhamelefs dalliance

Of wanton eyes; nor, ill-concealing it

Beneath the treach'rous cov'ring, tempt afide

The fecret glance, with meditated fraud.

Go now, and lay thy modeft garments by :

In naked beauty, mount thy milk-white fteed,

And through the ftreets, in face of open day,

And gazing flaves, their fair deliv'rer ride :

Then will I own thy pity was fincere,

Applaud thy virtue, and confirm thy fuit.

But if thou lik'ft not fuch ungentle terms,

And fure thy foul the guilty thought abhors !

Know then that Leofric, like thee, can feel,

Like thee, may pity, while he feems fevere,

And

And urge thy fuit no more.   His fpeech he clos'd,

And, with ftrange oaths, confirm'd the fad decree.

Again, within Godiva's gentle breaft

New tumults rofe.   At length her female fears

Gave way, and fweet humanity prevail'd.

Reluctant, but refolv'd, the matchlefs fair

Gives all her naked beauty to the fun;

Then mounts her milk-white fteed, and, thro' the
            ftreets,

Rides fearlefs; her difhevell'd hair a veil!

That o'er her beauteous limbs luxuriant flow'd,

Nurs'd long by Fate for this important day!

Proftrate to earth th' aftonifh'd vaffals bow,

Or to their inmoft privacies retire.

All, but one prying flave! who fondly hop'd,

With venial curiofity, to gaze

On fuch a wond'rous dame.   But foul difgrace

O'ertook the bold offender, and he ftands,

By juft decree, a fpectacle abhorr'd,

And lafting monument of fwift revenge

For thoughts impure, and beauty's injur'd charms.

                                    Ye

Ye guardians of her rights, fo nobly won !

Cherifh the Mufe, who firft in modern ftrains

Effay'd to fing your lovely * Patriot's fame,

Anxious to refcue from oblivious time

Such matchlefs virtue, her heroic deed

Illuftrate, and your gay proceffion grace.

* See DUGDALE's Antiquities of Warwickfhire.

It is pleafant enough to obferve, with what gravity the above-mentioned learned writer dwells on the praifes of this renown'd lady. " And now, before I proceed," fays he, " I have a word more to fay of the noble Countefs GODEVA, which is, that befides her devout advancement of that pious work of his, i. e. her hufband LEOFRIC, in this magnificent monaftery, viz. of Monks at COVENTRY, fhe gave her whole treafure thereto, and fent for fkilful goldfmiths, who, with all the gold and filver fhe had, made croffes, images of faints, and other curious ornaments." Which paffages may ferve as a fpecimen of the devotion and patriotifm of thofe times.

END OF BOOK THE SECOND.

F 4 EDGE-

to face page 72.

EDGE-HILL.

BOOK III.

AFTERNOON.

ARGUMENT TO BOOK THE THIRD.

A F T E R N O O N.

A G A I N, the Mufe her airy flight effays.
Will VILLERS, fkill'd alike in claffic fong,
Or, with a critic's eye, to trace the charms
Of Nature's beauteous fcenes, attend the lay?
Will he, accuftom'd to foft Latian climes,
As to their fofter numbers, deign awhile
To quit the Mantuan Bard's harmonious ftrain,
By fweet attraction of the theme allur'd?
The Latian Poet's fong is ftill the fame.

Not

Not fo the Latian fields.   The gentle Arts

That made thofe fields fo fair, when Gothic Rule,

And Superftition, with her bigot train,

Fixt there their gloomy feat, to this fair Ifle

Retir'd, with Freedom's gen'rous fons to dwell,

To grace her cities, and her fmiling plains

With plenty cloathe, and crown the rural toil.

    Nor hath he found, throughout thofe fpacious
        realms

Where ALBIS flows, and ISTER's ftately flood,

More verdant meads, or more fuperb remains

Of old magnificence, than his own fields

Difplay, where * CLINTON's venerable walls

In ruin, ftill their ancient grandeur tell.

    Requires there aught of learning's pompous aid

To prove that all this outward frame of things

Is what it feems, not unfubftantial air,

Ideal vifion, or a waking dream,

* The magnificent ruins of KENILWORTH CASTLE, built
by GEOFRY DE CLINTON, and more particularly defcribed
in the preceding book, belong to the Right Hon. the Earl
of CLARENDON, many years refident in ITALY, and Envoy
to moft of the Courts in GERMANY.

Without

Without exiftence, fave what Fancy gives?

Shall we, becaufe we ftrive in vain to tell

How Matter acts on incorporeal Mind,

Or how, when fleep has lock'd up ev'ry fenfe,

Or fevers rage, Imagination paints

Unreal fcenes, reject what fober fenfe,

And calmeft thought atteft? Shall we confound

States wholly diff'rent? Sleep with wakeful life?

Difeafe with health? This were to quit the day,

And feek our path at midnight.   To renounce

Man's fureft evidence, and idolize

Imagination.   Hence then banifh we

Thefe metaphyfic fubtleties, and mark

The curious ftructure of thefe vifual orbs,

The windows of the mind; fubftance how clear,

Aqueous, or cryftalline! through which the foul,

As thro' a glafs, all outward things furveys.

See, while the fun gilds, with his golden beam,

Yon' diftant pile, which HYDE, with care refin'd,

From plunder guards, its form how beautiful!

Anon fome cloud his radiance intercepts,

And all the fplendid object fades away.

Or,

Or, if fome incruftation o'er the fight

Its baleful texture fpread, like a clear lens,

With filth obfcur'd ! no more the fenfory,

Thro' the thick film, imbibes the chearful day,

' But cloud inftead, and ever-during night

Surround it.'   So, when on fome weighty truth

A beam of heav'nly light its luftre fheds,

To Reafon's eye it looks fupremely fair.

But if foul Paffion, or diftemper'd Pride,

Impede its fearch, or Phrenzy feize the brain,

Then Ignorance a gloomy darknefs fpreads,

Or Superftition, with mifhapen forms,

Erects its favage empire in the mind.

   The vulgar race of men, like herds that graze,

On Inftinct live, not knowing how they live ;

While Reafon fleeps, or waking ftoops to Senfe.

But fage Philofophy explores the caufe

Of each phænomenon of fight, or found,

Tafte, touch, or fmell; each organ's inmoft frame,

And correfpondence with external things :

Explains how diff'rent texture of their parts

Excites fenfations diff'rent, rough, or fmooth,

                                        Bitter,

Bitter, or fweet, fragrance, or noifome fcent :

How various ftreams of undulating air,

Thro' the ear's winding labyrinth convey'd,

Caufe all the vaft variety of founds.

Hence too the fubtle properties of light,

And fev'n-fold colour are diftinctly view'd

In the prifmatic glafs, and outward forms

Shewn fairly drawn, in miniature divine,

On the tranfparent eye's membraneous cell.

By combination hence of diff'rent orbs,

Convex, or concave, thro' their cryftal pores,

Tranfmitting varioufly the folar ray,

With line oblique, the telefcopic tube

Reveals the wonders of the ftarry fphere,

Worlds above worlds; or, in a fingle grain,

Or watry drop, the penetrative eye ·

Difcerns innumerable inhabitants

Of perfect ftructure, imperceptible

To naked view.   Hence each defect of fenfe

Obtains relief; hence to the palfy'd ear

New impulfe, vifion new to languid fight,

Surprize to both, and youthful joys reftor'd !

Cheap

Cheap is the blifs we never knew to want!

So gracelefs fpendthrifts wafte unthankfully

Thofe fums, which Merit often feeks in vain,

And Poverty wou'd kneel to call its own.

So objects, hourly feen, unheeded pafs,

At which the new-created fight would gaze

With exquifite delight.   Doubt ye this truth?

A tale fhall place it fairer to your view.

A youth * there was, a youth of lib'ral mind,

And fair proportion in each lineament

Of outward form; but dim fuffufion veil'd

His fightlefs orbs, which roll'd, and roll'd in vain

To find the blaze of day.   From infancy,

Till full maturity glow'd on his cheek,

The long, long night its gloomy empire held,

And mock'd each gentle effort, lotions,

Or cataplafms, by parental hands,

With fruitlefs care employ'd.   At length a Leech,

Of fkill profound, well-vers'd in optic lore,

* For the general fubject of the following ftory, fee the
TATLER, Numb. 55, and SMITH's OPTICS.

An

An arduous task devis'd aside to draw

The veil, which, like a cloud, hung o'er his sight,

And ope a lucid passage to the sun.

Instant the Youth the promis'd blessing craves.

But first his parents, with uplifted hands,

The healing Pow'rs invoke, and pitying friends

With sympathizing heart, the rites prepare:

'Mongst these, who well deserv'd the important trust,

A gentle Maid there was, that long had wail'd

His hapless fate.   Full many a tedious hour

Had she, with converse, and instructive song,

Beguil'd.   Full many a step darkling her arm

Sustain'd him ; and, as they their youthful days

In friendly deeds, and mutual intercourse

Of sweet endearment pass'd, love in each breast

His empire fix'd ; in her's with pity join'd,

In his with gratitude, and deep regard.

The friendly wound was giv'n ; th' obstructing film

Drawn artfully aside ; and, on his sight

Burst the full tide of day.   Surpriz'd he stood,

Not knowing where he was, nor what he saw !

The skilful artist first, as first in place

G   He

He view'd, then feiz'd his hand, then felt his own,

Then mark'd their near refemblance, much perplex'd,

And ftill the more perplex'd, the more he faw.

Now filence firft th' impatient mother broke,

And, as her eager looks on him fhe bent,

" My fon," fhe cried, " my fon !" On her he gaz'd

With frefh furprize. And, what? he cried, art thou

My mother? for thy voice befpeaks thee fuch,

Tho' to my fight unknown. Thy mother I!

She quick reply'd, thy fifter, brother thefe—

O! 'tis too much, he faid; too foon to part,

Ere well we meet! But this new flood of day

O'erpow'rs me, and I feel a death-like damp

Chill all my frame, and ftop my fault'ring tongue.

Now Lydia, fo they call'd his gentle friend,

Who, with averted eye, but, in her foul,

Had felt the lancing fteel, her aid apply'd,

And ftay, dear youth, fhe faid, or with thee take

Thy Lydia, thine alike in life, or death.

At Lydia's name, at Lydia's well-known voice,

He ftrove again to raife his drooping head,

, And

And ope his clofing eye, but ftrove in vain,
And on her trembling bofom funk away.   '

　　Now other fears diftraƈt his weeping friends.
But fhort this grief! for foon his life return'd,
And, with return of life, return'd their peace.
Yet, for his fafety, they refolve awhile
His infant fenfe from day's bright beams to guard,
Ere yet again they tempt fuch dang'rous joy.

　　As, when from fome tranfporting dream awak'd,
We fondly on the fweet delufion dwell,
And, with intenfe refleƈtion, to our minds
Piƈture th' enchanted fcene—angelic forms—
Converfe fublime—and more than waking blifs!
Till the coy vifion, as the more we ftrive
To paint it livelier on th' enraptur'd fenfe,
Still fainter grows, and dies at laft away:
So dwelt the Youth on his late tranfient joy,
So long'd the dear remembrance to renew.

　　At length, *again* the wifh'd-for day arriv'd.
The tafk was LYDIA's! her's the charge, *alone*
From dangers new to guard the dear delight;
But firft th' impatient Youth fhe thus addrefs'd.

Dear

Dear Youth! my trembling hands but ill effay
This tender tafk, and, with unufual fear,
My flutt'ring heart forebodes fome danger nigh.

Difmifs thy fears, he cried, nor think fo ill
I con thy leffons, as ftill need be taught
To hail, with caution, the new-coming day.
Then loofe thefe envious folds, and teach my fight,
If more can be, to make thee more belov'd.

Ah! there's my grief, fhe cried: 'tis true our hearts
With mutual paffion burn, but then 'tis true
Thou ne'er haft known me by that fubtle fenfe
Thro' which love moft an eafy paffage finds ;
That fenfe! which foon may fhew thee many a maid
Fairer than Lydia, tho' more faithful none.
And may fhe not ceafe then to be belov'd ?
May fhe not then, when lefs thou need'ft her care,
Give place to fome new charmer ? 'Tis for this
I figh ; for this my fad foreboding fears
New terrors form.   And can'ft thou then, he cried,
Want aught that might endear thee to my foul ?
Art thou not excellence ? Art thou not all
That man cou'd wifh ? Goodnefs, and gentleft love ?

Can

Can I forget thy long affiduous care?

Thy morning-tendance, fureft mark to me

Of day's return, of night thy late adieu?

Do I need aught to make my blifs compleat,

When thou art by me? when I prefs thy hand?

When I breath fragrance at thy near approach;

And hear the fweeteft mufic in thy voice?

Can that, which to each other fenfe is dear,

So wond'rous dear, be otherwife to fight?

Or can fight make, what is to reafon good,

And lovely, feem lefs lovely, and lefs good?

Perifh the fenfe, that wou'd make LYDIA fuch!

Perifh its joys, thofe joys however great!

If to be purchas'd with the lofs of thee,

O my dear LYDIA! if there be indeed

The danger thou report'ft, O! by our love,

Our mutual love, I charge thee, ne'er unbind

Thefe haplefs orbs, or tear them from their feat,

Ere they betray me thus to worfe than death:

No, Heav'n forbid! fhe cried, for Heav'n hath heard

Thy parents pray'rs, and many a friend now waits

To mingle looks of cordial love with thine.

And fhou'd I rob them of the facred blifs?

Shou'd I deprive thee of the rapt'rous fight?

No! be thou happy; happy be thy friends;

Whatever fate attends thy LYDIA's love;

Thy haplefs LYDIA!—Haplefs did I fay?

Ah! wherefore? wherefore wrong I thus thy worth?

Why doubt thy well-known truth, and conftant mind?

No, happieft fhe of all the happy train,

In mutual vows, and plighted faith fecure!

So faying, fhe the filken bandage loos'd,

Nor added further fpeech, prepar'd to watch

The new furprize, and guide the doubtful fcene,

By filence more than tenfold night conceal'd.

When thus the Youth.   And is this then the world,

In which I am to live?   Am I awake?

Or do I dream? Or hath fome pow'r unknown,

Far from my friends, far from my native home;

Convey'd me to thefe radiant feats?   O thou I·

Inhabitant of this enlighten'd world!

Whofe heav'nly foftnefs far tranfcends his fhape,

By whom this miracle was firft atchiev'd,

O! deign thou to inftruct me where I am;

3   And

And how to name thee by true character,

Angel, or mortal! Once I had a friend,

Who, but till now, ne'er left me in diftrefs.

Her fpeech was harmony, at which my heart

With tranfport flutter'd; and her gracious hand

Supplied me with whate'er my wifh cou'd form;

Supply, and tranfport ne'er fo wifh'd before!

Never, when wanted, yet, fo long denied!

Why is fhe filent now, when moft I long

To hear her heav'nly voice? why flies fhe not

With more than ufual fpeed to crown my blifs?

Ah! did I leave her in that darkfome world?

Or rather dwells fhe not in thefe bright realms,

Companion fit for fuch fair forms as thine?

O! teach me, if thou canft, how I may find

This gentle counfellor; when found, how know

By this new fenfe, which, better ftill to rate

Her worth, I chiefly wifh'd. The lovely form

Replied, In me behold that gentle friend,

If ftill thou own'ft me fuch. O! yes, 'tis fhe,

He cried; 'tis LYDIA! 'tis her charming voice!

O! fpeak again; O! let me prefs thy hand:

On

On thefe I can rely.   This new-born fenfe

May cheat me.   Yet fo much I prize thy form,

I willingly wou'd think it tells me true—

    Ha! what are thefe?   Are they not they, of whom

Thou warn'dft me?   Yes—true—they are beautiful.

But have they lov'd like thee, like thee convers'd?

They move not as we move, they bear no part

In my new blifs.   And yet methinks, in one,

Her form I can defcry, tho' now fo calm!

Who call'd me fon.   Miftaken Youth!   fhe cried,

Thefe are not what they feem; are not as we,

Not living fubftances, but pictur'd fhapes,

Refemblances of life! by mixture form'd

Of light, and fhade, in fweet proportion join'd.

But hark! I hear, without, thy longing friends,

Who wait my fummons, and reprove my ftay.

    To thy direction, cried th' enraptur'd Youth,

To thy direction I commit my fteps.

Lead on, be thou my guide, as late, fo now,

In this new world, and teach me how to ufe

This wond'rous faculty; which thus, fo foon

Mocks me with phantoms.   Yet enough for me!

                        That

That all my paft experience joins with this

To tell me I am happier than I know.

To tell me thou art Lydia ! From whofe fide

I never more will part ! with whom compar'd,

All others of her fex, however fair,

Shall be like painted, unfubftantial forms.

So when the foul, inflam'd with ftrong defire

Of purer blifs, its earthly manfion leaves,

Perhaps fome friendly genius, wont to fteer

With minifterial charge, his dang'rous fteps ;

Perhaps fome gentle partner of his toil,

More early bleft, in radiant luftre clad,

And form celeftial, meets his dazzled fight ;

And guides his way, thro' tracklefs fields of air,

To join, with rapt'rous joy, 'th' ethereal train.

Now to the midland fearch the Mufe returns.

For more, and ftill more bufy fcenes remain ;

The promis'd fchools of wife artificers

In brafs, and iron.   But another fchool

Of gentler arts demands the Mufe's fong,

Where firft fhe learn'd to fcan the meafur'd verfe,

And aukwardly her infant notes effay'd.

Hail

Hail SOLIHUL! refpectful I falute

Thy walls; more awful once! when, from the fweets

Of feftive freedom, and domeftic eafe,

With throbbing heart, to the ftern difcipline

Of pædagogue morofe I fad return'd.

But tho' no more his brow fevere, nor dread

Of birchen fceptre awes my riper age,

A fterner tyrant rifes to my view,

With deadlier weapon arm'd. Ah! *Critic!* fpare,

O! fpare the Mufe, who feels her youthful fears

On thee transfer'd, and trembles at thy lafh.

Againft the venal tribe, that proftitutes

The tuneful art, to footh the villain's breaft,

To blazon fools, or feed the pamper'd luft

Of bloated vanity; againft the tribe

Which cafts its wanton jefts at holy truths,

Or clothes, with virtue's garb, th' accurfed train

Of loathfome vices, lift thy vengeful arm,

And all thy juft feverity exert.

Enough to venial faults, and haplefs want

Of animated numbers, fuch as breathe

The

The foul of epic fong, hath erſt been paid
Within theſe walls, ſtill ſtain'd with infant blood.

Yet may I not forget the pious care
Of love parental, anxious to improve
My youthful mind.   Nor yet the debt diſown
Due to ſevere reſtraint, and rigid laws,
The wholeſome curb of Paſſion's headſtrong reign.
To them I owe that ere, with painful toil,
Thro' PRISCIAN's crabbed rules, laborious taſk!
I held my courſe, till the dull, tireſome road
Plac'd me on *claſſic* ground, that well repaid
The labours of the way.   To them I owe
The pleaſing knowledge of my youthful mates
Matur'd in age, and honours.   Theſe among,
I gratulate whom AUGUSTA's ſenate hails
Father! and, in each charge, and high employ,
Found worthy all her love, with ampleſt truſt,
And dignity inveſts.   And well I ween,
Her tribunitial pow'r, and purple pomp
On thee confers, in living manners ſchool'd
To guard her weal, and vindicate her rights,
O LADBROKE! once in the ſame fortunes claſs'd

Of

Of early life; with count'nance uneftrang'd,

For ev'ry friendly deed ftill vacant found!

Nor can the Mufe, while fhe thefe fcenes furveys,

Forget her SHENSTONE, in the youthful toil

Affociate; whofe bright dawn of genius oft

Smooth'd my incondite verfe; whofe friendly voice

Call'd me from giddy fports to follow him

Intent on better themes—call'd me to tafte

The charms of Britifh fong, the pictur'd page

Admire, or mark his imitative fkill;

Or with him range in folitary fhades,

And fcoop rude grottos in the fhelving bank.

Such were the joys that cheer'd life's early morn!

Such the ftrong fympathy of foul, that knit

Our hearts congenial in fweet amity!

On CHERWEL's banks, by kindred fcience nurs'd;

And well-matur'd in life's advancing ftage,

When, on ARDENNA's plain, we fondly ftray'd,

With mutual truft, and amicable thought;

Or in the focial circle gaily join'd:

Or round his Leafowe's happy circuit rov'd;

On hill, and dale invoking ev'ry Mufe,

                                        Nor

Nor Tempe's fhade, nor Aganippe's fount
Envied ; fo willingly the Dryads nurs'd
His groves ; fo lib'rally their cryftal urns
The Naiads pour'd, enchanted with his fpells ;
And pleas'd to fee their ever-flowing ftreams
Led by his hand, in many a mazy line ;
Or, in the copious tide, collected large,
Or tumbling from the rock, in fportive falls,
Now, from the lofty bank, precipitate ;
And now, in gentler courfe, with murmurs foft
Soothing the ear ; and now, in concert join'd,
Fall above fall, oblique, and intricate,
Among the twifted roots.   Ah ! whilft I write,
In deeper murmur flows the fadning ftream ;
Wither the groves ; and from the beauteous fcene,
Its foft enchantments fly.   No more for me
A charm it wears, fince he alas ! is gone,
Whofe genius plann'd it, and whofe fpirit grac'd.
Ah ! hourly does the fatal doom, pronounc'd
Againft rebellious fin, fome focial band
Diffolve, and leave a thoufand friends to weep,
Soon fuch themfelves, as thofe they now lament !

This

This mournful tribute to thy mem'ry paid!

The Muse pursues her solitary way ;

But heavily pursues, since thou art gone,

Whose counsel brighten'd, and whose friendship shar'd

The pleasing task.   Now BREMICHAM! to thee

She steers her flight, and, in thy busy scenes,

Seeks to restrain awhile the starting tear.

   Yet ere her song describes the smoky forge,

Or sounding anvil, to the dusky heath

Her gentle train she leads.   What ? tho' no grain,

Or herbage sweet, or waving woods adorn

Its dreary surface, yet it bears, within,

A richer treasury.   So worthy minds

Oft lurk beneath a rude, unsightly form.

More hapless they ! that few observers search,

Studious to find this intellectual ore,

And stamp, with gen'rous deed, its current worth.

Here many a merchant turns adventurer,

Encourag'd, not disgusted.   Interest thus,

On sordid minds, with stronger impulse works,

Than virtue's heav'nly flame.   Yet Providence

Converts to gen'ral use man's selfish ends.

                                        Hence

Hence are the hungry fed, the naked cloath'd,

The wintry damps difpell'd, and focial mirth

Exults, and glows before the blazing hearth.

  When likely figns th' adventrous fearch invite,

A cunning artift tries the latent foil :

And if his fubtle engine, in return,

A brittle mafs contains of fable hue,

Strait he prepares th' obftructing earth to clear,

And raife the crumbling rock.   A narrow pafs

Once made, wide, and more wide the gloomy cave

Stretches its vaulted ifles, by num'rous hands

Hourly extended.   Some the pick-axe ply,

Loos'ning the quarry from its native bed.

Some waft it into light.   Thus the grim ore,

Here ufelefs, like the mifer's brighter hoard,

Is from its prifon brought, and fent abroad,

The frozen hours to cheer, to minifter

To needful fuftenance, and polifh'd arts.

Mean while the fubterraneous city fpreads

Its covert ftreets, and echoes with the noife

Of fwarthy flaves, and inftruments of toil.

They, fuch the force of Cuftom's pow'rful laws !

Purfue

Purfue their footy labours, deftitute

Of the fun's cheering light, and genial warmth.

And oft a chilling damp, or unctuous mift,

Loos'd from the crumbly caverns, iffues forth,

Stopping the fprings of life. And oft the flood,

Diverted from its courfe, in torrents pours,

Drowning the nether world. To cure thefe ills

Philofophy two curious arts fupplies,

To drain th' imprifon'd air, and, in its place,

More pure convey, or, with impetuous force,

To raife the gath'ring torrents from the deep.

One from the * wind its falutary pow'r

Derives, thy charity to fick'ning crowds,

From cheerful haunts, and Nature's balmy draughts

Confin'd; O friend of man, illuftrious † Hales!

That, ftranger ftill! its influence owes to air ‡,

By cold, and heat alternate now condens'd,

Now rarefied ‖. Agent! to vulgar thought

---

* The Ventilator.

† Dr. Stephen Hales.

‡ The Fire-engine.

‖ " Denfat erant quæ rara modo, et quæ denfa relaxat."

How

How feeming weak, in act how pow'rful feen!
So Providence, by inftruments defpis'd,
All human force, and policy confounds.

But who that fiercer element can rule?
When, in the nitrous cave, the kindling flame,
By pitchy vapours fed, from cell to cell,
With fury fpreads; and the wide fewell'd earth,
Around, with greedy joy, receives the blaze.
By its own entrails nourifh'd, like thofe mounts
Vefuvian, or Æthean, ftill it waftes,
And ftill new fewel for its rapine finds
Exhauftlefs.   Wretched he! who journeying late,
O'er the parch'd heath, bewilder'd, feeks his way,
Oft will his fnorting fteed, with terror ftruck,
His wonted fpeed refufe, or ftart afide,
With rifing fmoak, and ruddy flame annoy'd.
While, at each ftep, his trembling rider quakes,
Appall'd with thoughts of bog, or cavern'd pit,
Or treach'rous earth, fubfiding where they tread,
Tremendous paffage to the realms of death!

Yet want there not ev'n here fome lucid fpots
The fmoaky fcene to cheer, and, by contraft,

More fair.   Such DARTMOUTH's cultivated * lawns!

Himself, diftinguifh'd more with ornament

Of cultur'd manners, and fupernal light!

Such † thine, O BRIDGMAN! Such—but envious time

Forbids the Mufe to thefe fair fcenes to rove,

Still minding her of her unfinifh'd theme,

From ruffet heaths, and fmould'ring furnaces,

To trace the progrefs of thy fteely arts,

‡ *Queen of the founding anvil!* ASTON ‖ thee,

And § EDGBASTON with hofpitable fhade,

And rural pomp inveft.   O! warn thy fons;

When, for a time, their labours they forget,

Not to moleft thefe peaceful folitudes.

So may the mafters of the beauteous fcene,

Protect thy commerce, and their toil reward.

* SANDWEL, the feat of the Right Hon. the Earl of DARTMOUTH.

† CASTLE-BROMWICK, the feat of Sir HENRY BRIDGMAN, Bart.

‡ BREMICHAM, alias BIRMINGHAM.

‖ The feat of Sir LISTER HOLT, Bart.

§ The feat of Sir HENRY GOUGH, Bart.

Nor

Nor does the barren foil conceal alone
The fable rock inflammable.   Oft-times
More pond'rous ore beneath its furface lies,
Compact, metallic, but with earthy parts
Incrufted.   Thefe the fmoaky kiln confumes,
And to the furnace's impetuous rage
Configns the folid ore.   In the fierce heat
The pure diffolves, the drofs remains behind.
This pufh'd afide, the trickling metal flows
Thro' fecret valves along the channel'd floor,
Where in the mazy moulds of figur'd fand,
Anon it hardens.   Now the bufy forge
Reiterates its blows, to form the bar
Large, maffy, ftrong.   Another art expands,
Another yet divides the yielding mafs
To many a taper length, fit to receive
The artift's will, and take its deftin'd form.

    Soon o'er thy furrow'd pavement, Bremicham!
Ride the loofe bars obftrep'rous; to the fons
Of languid fenfe, and frame too delicate
Harfh noife perchance, but harmony to thine.

Inftant innumerable hands prepare
To fhape, and mould the malleable ore.
Their heavy fides th' inflated bellows heave,
Tugged by the pulley'd line, and, with their blaft
Continuous, the fleeping embers roufe,
And kindle into life.   Strait the rough mafs,
Plung'd in the blazing hearth, its heat contracts,
And glows tranfparent.   Now, CYCLOPEAN chief!
Quick on the anvil lay the burning bar,
And with thy lufty fellows, on its fides
Imprefs the weighty ftroke.   See, how they ftrain
The fwelling nerve, and lift the finewy * arm
In meafur'd time; while with their clatt'ring blows,
From ftreet to ftreet the propagated found
Increafing echoes, and, on ev'ry fide,
The tortur'd metal fpreads a radiant fhow'r.

'Tis noife, and hurry all! The thronged ftreet,
The clofe-piled warehoufe, and the bufy fhop!

---

* " Illi inter fefe magnâ vi brachia tollunt
  " In numerum, verfantque tenaci forcipe ferrum.
                                   VIRG.

                                   With

With nimble ftroke the tinkling hammers move;

While flow, and weighty the vaft fledge defcends,

In folemn bafe refponfive, or apart,

Or focially conjoin'd in tuneful peal.

The rough file * grates; yet ufeful is its touch,

As fharp corrofives to the fchirrhous flefh,

Or, to the ftubborn temper, keen rebuke.

How the coarfe metal brightens into fame

Shap'd by their plaftic hands ! what ornament !

What various ufe ! See there the glitt'ring knife

Of temper'd edge ! The fciffars' double fhaft,

Ufelefs apart, in focial union join'd,

Each aiding each ! Emblem how beautiful

Of happy nuptial leagues ! The button round,

Plain, or imboft, or bright with fteely rays !

Or oblong buckle, on the lacker'd fhoe,

With polifh'd luftre, bending elegant

Its fhapely rim.   But who can count the forms

* " Tum ferri rigor, et argutæ lamina ferræ,
  " Tum variæ venere artes, &c."

                                        Virg.

H 3   That

That hourly from the glowing embers rife,

Or fhine attractive thro' the glitt'ring pane,

And emulate their parent fires? what art

* Can, in the fcanty bounds of meafur'd verfe,

Difplay the treafure of a thoufand mines

To wond'rous fhapes by ftubborn labour wrought?

Nor this alone thy praife.   Of various grains

Thy fons a compound form, and to the fire

Commit the precious mixture, if perchance

Some glitt'ring mafs may blefs their midnight toil,

Or gloffy varnifh, or enamel fair,

To fhame the pride of China, or Japan.

Nor wanting is the graver's pointed fteel,

Nor pencil, wand'ring o'er the polifh'd plate,

With glowing tints, and mimic life endued.

Thine too, of graceful form, the letter'd type!

The friend of learning, and the poet's pride!

Without thee what avail his fplendid aims,

---

* " Sed neque quàm multæ fpecies, nec nomina quæ fint,
  " Eft numerus: neque enim numero comprêndere refert."
                                                    Virg.

And

And midnight labours? Painful drudgery!
And pow'rlefs effort! But that thought of thee
Imprints frefh vigour on his panting breaft,
As thou ere long fhalt on his work imprefs;
And, with immortal fame, his praife repay.

   Hail, native Britifh Ore! of thee poffefs'd,
We envy not GOLCONDA's fparkling mines,
Nor thine POTOSI! nor thy kindred hills,
Teeming with gold. What? tho' in outward form
Lefs fair? not lefs thy worth. To thee we owe
More riches than Peruvian mines can yield,
Or MOTEZUMA's crowded magazines,
And palaces cou'd boaft, though roof'd with gold.
Splendid barbarity! and rich diftrefs!
Without the focial arts, and ufeful toil;
That polifh life, and civilize the mind!
Thefe are thy gifts, which gold can never buy.

   Thine is the praife to cultivate the foil;
To bare its inmoft ftrata to the fun;
To break, and meliorate the ftiffen'd clay,
And, from its clofe confinement, fet at large
Its vegetative virtue. Thine it is

The with'ring hay, and ripen'd grain to sheer,
And waft the joyous harvest round the land,

Go now, and see if, to the Silver's edge,
The reedy stalk will yield its bearded store,
In weighty sheafs.   Or if the stubborn marle,
In sidelong rows, with easy force will rise
Before the Silver plowshare's glitt'ring point.
Or wou'd your gen'rous horses tread more safe
On plated Gold?   Your wheels, with swifter force
On golden axles move?   Then grateful own,
Britannia's sons! Heav'n's providential love,
That gave you real wealth, not wealth in shew,
Whose price in bare imagination lies,
And artificial compact.   Thankful ply
Your Iron arts, and rule the vanquish'd world.

Hail, native Ore! without thy pow'rful aid,
We still had liv'd in huts, with the green sod,
And broken branches roof'd.   Thine is the plane,
The chissel thine; which shape the well-arch'd dome,
The graceful portico; and sculptur'd walls.

Wou'd ye your coarse, unsightly mines exchange
For Mexiconian hills? to tread on gold,

As

As vulgar fand? with naked limbs, to brave
The cold, bleak air? to urge the tedious chace,
By painful hunger ftung, with artlefs toil,
Thro' gloomy forefts, where the founding axe,
To the fun's beam, ne'er op'd the cheerful glade,
Nor culture's healthful face was ever feen?
In fqualid huts to lay your weary limbs,
Bleeding, and faint, and ftrangers to the blifs
Of home-felt eafe, which Britifh fwains can earn,
With a bare fpade; but ill alas! cou'd earn,
With fpades of gold? Such the poor Indian's lot!
Who ftarves 'midft gold, like mifers o'er their bags;
Not with like guilt!   Hail, native Britifh Ore!
For thine is trade, that with its various ftores,
Sails round the world, and vifits ev'ry clime,
And makes the treafures of each clime her own,
By gainful commerce of her woolly vefts,
Wrought by the fpiky comb; or fteely wares,
From the coarfe mafs, by ftubborn toil, refin'd.
Such are thy peaceful gifts!   And War to thee
Its beft fupport, and deadlieft horror owes,

The

The glitt'ring faulchion, and the thund'ring tube !
At whose tremendous gleam, and volley'd fire,
Barbarian kings fly from their useless hoards,
And yield them all to thy superior pow'r.

END OF BOOK THE THIRD.

EDGE-

to face page 107.

EDGE-HILL.

BOOK IV.

EVENING.

ARGUMENT TO BOOK THE FOURTH.

Evening Walk along the Hill to the N. E. Point. Scene from thence. DASSET-HILLS. FARNBOROUGH. WORMLEIGHTON. SHUCKBURG. LEAME *and* ICHENE. *Places near those two Rivers.* BENNONES, *or* HIGH-CROSS. FOSS-WAY. WATLING-STREET. *Inland Navigation. Places of Note. Return. Panegyric on the Country. The Scene moralized. Tho' beautiful, yet transient. Change by Approach of Winter. Of Storms and Pestilential Seasons. Murrain. Rot amongst the Sheep. General Thoughts on the Vanity and Disorders of human Life. Battle of* EDGE-HILL. *Reflections. Conclusion.*

BOOK IV.

E V E N I N G.

IN purple veſtments clad, the temper'd ſky
 Invites us from our hoſpitable roof,
To taſte her influence mild; while to the weſt
The jocund ſun his radiant chariot drives,
With rapid courſe, untir'd. Ye nymphs, and ſwains!
Now quit the ſhade, and, with recruited ſtrength,
Along the yet untroden terrace urge
Your vig'rous ſteps. With moderated heat,

And

And ray oblique, the fun fhall not o'erpow'r;
But kindly aid your yet unfinifh'd fearch.

Not after fable night, in filence hufh'd,
More welcome is th' approach of op'ning morn;
' With fong of early birds,' than the frefh breeze
Of foften'd air fucceeding fultry heat,
And the wild tumult of the buzzing day.

Nor think, tho' much is paft, that nought remains,
Or nought of beauty, or attractive worth,
Save what the morning-fun, or noon-tide ray,
Hath, with his rifing beam, diftinctly mark'd,
Or more confus'dly, with meridian blaze,
Daz'ling difplay'd imperfect.   Downward he
Shall other hills illumine oppofite,
And other vales as beauteous as the paft;
Suggefting to the Mufe new argument,
And frefh inftruction for her clofing lay.

There Dasset's ridgy mountain courts the fong.
Scarce Malvern boafts his adverfe boundary
More graceful.   Like the tempeft-driven wave,
Irregularly great, his bare tops brave

The

The winds, and, on his fides, the fat'ning ox

Crops the rich verdure.   When at Hastings' field,

The Norman Conqueror a kingdom won

In this fair Ifle, and to another race

The Saxon pow'r transferr'd ; an alien * lord,

Companion of his toil ! by fov'reign grant,

Thefe airy fields obtain'd.   Now the tall Mount,

By claim more juft, a nobler mafter owns ;

To tyrant force, and flavifh laws a foe.

But happier lands, near Ouse's reedy fhore,

(What leifure ardent love of public weal

Permits) his care employ ; where Nature's charms

With learned Art combin'd ; the richeft domes,

And faireft lawns, adorn'd with ev'ry grace

Of beauty, or magnificent defign,

By Cobham's eye approv'd, or Grenville plann'd,

The villas of imperial Rome outvie ;

And form a fcene of ftatelier pomp—a Stowe.

Her walls the living boaft, *thefe* boaft the dead,

Beneath their roof, in facred duft entomb'd.

* The Earl of Mellent.

Lie light, O earth ! on that illuſtrious Dame *,

Who, from her own prolific womb deriv'd,

To people thy green orb, ſucceſſive ſaw

Sev'n times an hundred births.   A goodlier train !

Than that, with which the Patriarch journey'd erſt

From PADAN-ARAM, to the Mamrean plains :

Or that more num'rous, which, with large increaſe,

At JOSEPH's call, in wond'rous caravans,

Reviving ſight ! by Heav'n's decree prepar'd,

He led to GOSHEN, EGYPT's fruitful ſoil.

Where the tall pillar lifts its taper head,

Her ſpacious terrace, and ſurrounding lawns,

Deckt with no ſparing coſt of planted tufts,

Or ornamented building, † FARNBOROUGH boaſts.

Hear they her maſter's call ? in ſturdy troops,

The jocund labourers hie, and, at his nod,

A thouſand hands or ſmooth the ſlanting hill,

* Dame HESTER TEMPLE, of whom this is recorded by
FULLER, in his account of BUCKINGHAMSHIRE, and who
lies buried, with many of that ancient family, in the pariſh-
church of BURTON-DASSET.

† The ſeat of WILLIAM HOLBECH, Eſq.

Or

Or fcoop new channels for the gath'ring flood,

And, in his pleafures, find fubftantial blifs.

   Nor fhall thy verdant paftures be unfung.

* WORMLEIGHTON! erft th' abode of SPENSER's

    race,

Their title now! What? tho' in height thou yield'ft

To DASSET, not in fweet luxuriance

Of fatning herbage, or of rifing groves;

Beneath whofe fhade the lufty fteers repofe

Their cumbrous limbs, mixt with the woolly tribes,

And leifurely concoct their graffy meal.

   Her wood-capt fummit † SHUCKBURGH there dif-

    plays;

Nor fears neglect, in her own worth fecure,

And glorying in the name her mafter bears.

Nor will her fcenes, with clofer eye, furvey'd,

Fruftrate the fearcher's toil, if fteepy hills,

By frequent chafms disjoin'd, and glens profound,

   * An eftate, and ancient feat, belonging to the Right
Hon. Earl SPENSER.

   † The feat of Sir CH. SHUCKBURGH, Bart.

And

And broken precipices, vaſt, and rude

Delight the ſenſe; or Nature's leſſer works,

Tho' leſſer, not leſs fair! or native ſtone,

Or fiſh, the little * Aſtroit's doubtful race,

For ſtarry rays, and pencil'd ſhades admir'd!

Invite him to theſe fields, their airy bed.

Where LEAME and ICHENE own a kindred riſe,

And haſte their neighb'ring currents to unite,

New hills ariſe, new paſtures green, and fields

With other harveſts crown'd; with other charms

Villas, and towns with other arts adorn'd.

There ICHINGTON its downward ſtructures views

In ICHENE's paſſing wave, which, like the Mole,

Her ſubterraneous journey long purſues,

Ere to the ſun ſhe gives her lucid ſtream.

Thy villa, † LEAMINGTON! her ſiſter nymph

In her fair boſom ſhews; while, on her banks,

As further ſhe her liquid courſe purſues,

* The Aſtroites, or Star-ſtones, found here.

† The ſeat of Sir WILLIAM WHEELER, Bart.

Amidſt

Amidft furrounding woods his ancient walls

* Birb'ry conceals, and triumphs in the fhade.

Not fuch thy lot, O † Bourton ! nor from fight

Retireft thou, but, with complacent fmile,

Thy focial afpect courts the diftant eye,

And views the diftant fcene reciprocal,

Delighting, and delighted.   Dufky heaths

Succeed, as oft to mirth, the gloomy hour !

Leading th' unfinifh'd fearch to thy fam'd feat

‡ Bennones! where two military ways

Each other crofs, tranfverfe from fea to fea,

The Romans hoftile paths!   There § Newnham's
         walls

With graceful pride afcend, th' inverted pile

In her clear ftream, with flow'ry margin grac'd,

Admiring.   ‖ Newbold there her modeft charms

* The feat of Sir Theophilus Biddulph, Bart.

† The feat of John Shuckburgh, Efq.

‡ A Roman ftation, where the Fofs-Way and Watling-
ftreet crofs each other.

§ The feat of the Right Hon. the Earl of Denbeigh.

‖ The feat of Sir Francis Skipwith, Bart.

More bafhfully unveils, with folemn woods,

And verdant glades enamour'd.   Here her lawns,

And rifing groves for future fhelter form'd,

Fair * Coton wide difplays.   There Addison,

With mind ferene, his moral theme revolv'd,

Inftruction dreft in Learning's faireft form!

The graveft wifdom with the livelieft wit

Attemper'd! or, beneath thy roof retir'd

O † Bilton! much of peace, and liberty

Sublimely mus'd, on Britain's weal intent,

Or in thy fhade the coy Pierians woo'd.

   Another theme demands the varying fong.

Lo! where but late the flocks, and heifers graz'd,

Or yellow harvefts wav'd, now, thro' the vale,

Or o'er the plain, or round the flanting hill

A glitt'ring path attracts the gazer's eye,

Where footy barques purfue their liquid track

Thro' lawns, and woods, and villages remote

From public haunt, which wonder as they pafs.

* The feat of Dixwell Grimes, Efq.

† The feat of the Right Hon. Joseph Addison, Efq.

The

The channel'd road ftill onward moves, and ftill
With level courfe, the flood attendant leads.
Hills, dales oppofe in vain.   A thoufand hands
Now thro' the mountain's fide a paffage ope,
Now with ftupendous arches bridge the vale,
Now over paths, and rivers urge their way
Aloft in air.   Again the Roman pride
Beneath thy fpacious camp embattled hill,
O * BRINKLOW ! feems with gentler arts return'd.
But BRITAIN now no bold invader fears,
No foreign aid invokes.   Alike in arts
Of peace, or war renown'd.   Alike in both
She rivals ancient ROME's immortal fame.

    Still villas fair, and populous towns remain—
POLESWORTH, and ATHERSTONE, and EATON's walls
To charity devote ! and, TAMWORTH, thine

---

    * The Canal defign'd for a communication between the
Cities of OXFORD and COVENTRY, paffes through BRINK-
LOW, where is a magnificent aquedu&t, confifting of twelve
arches, with a high bank of earth at each end, croffing a
valley beneath the veftiges of a Roman camp, and tumulus,
on the Fofs-Way.

I 3   To

To martial fame! and thine, O * MERIVAL!

Boasting thy beauteous woods, and lofty scite!

† And COLESHILL! long for momentary date

Of human life, tho' for our wishes short,

Repose of DIGBY's honourable age!

   Nor may the Muse, tho' on her homeward way

Intent, short space refuse his alleys green,

And decent walls with due respect to greet

‡ On BLYTHE's fair stream, to whose laborious toil

She many a lesson owes, his painful search

Enjoying without pain, and, at her ease,

With equal love of native soil inspir'd,

Singing in measur'd phrase her country's fame.

   § Nor, ARBURY! may we thy scenes forget,

   * The seat of the late EDWARD STRATFORD, Esq; an extersive view to Charley Forest and Bosworth Field.

   † Seat of the late Right Hon. Lord DIGBY, commonly called, the good Lord DIGBY.

   ‡ BLYTHE HALL, the seat of Sir WILLIAM DUGDALE, now belonging to RICHARD GEAST, Esq.

   § The seat of Sir ROGER NEWDIGATE, Bart. Member of Parliament for the University of Oxford.

Haunt

Haunt of the Naiads, and each woodland nymph!

Rejoicing in his care, to whom adorn'd

With all the graces which her fchools expound,

The gowny fons of Isis truft their own,

And Britain's weal.   Nor fhall thy fplendid walls,

O * Packington! allure the Mufe in vain.

The Goths no longer here their empire hold.

The fhaven terrac'd hill, flope above flope,

And high impris'ning walls to Belgia's coaft

Their native clime retire.—In formal bounds

The long canal no more confines the ftream

Reluctant.—Trees no more their tortur'd limbs

Lament—no more the long-neglected fields,

Like outlaws banifh'd for fome vile offence,

Are hid from fight—from its proud refervoir

Of ampleft fize, and fair indented form,

Along the channel'd lawn the copious ftream

With winding grace the ftately current leads.

The channel'd lawn its bounteous ftream repays,

With ever-verdant banks, and cooling fhades,

* The feat of the Right Hon. the Earl of Aylesford.

I 4   And

And wand'ring paths, that emulate its courfe.

On ev'ry fide fpreads wide the beauteous fcene,

Affemblage fair of plains, and hills, and woods,

And plants of od'rous fcent—plains, hills, and woods,

And od'rous plants rejoice, and fmiling hail

The reign of Nature, while attendant Art

Submiffive waits to cultivate her charms.

  Hail happy land! which Nature's partial fmile

Hath robed profufely gay! whofe champaigns wide

With plenteous harvefts wave; whofe paftures fwarm

With horned tribes, or the fheep's fleecy race;

To the thronged fhambles yielding wholefome food,

And various labour to man's active pow'rs,

Not lefs benign than to the weary reft.

Nor deftitute thy woodland fcenes of wealth,

Or fylvan beauty! there the lordly fwain

His fcantier fields improves; o'er his own realms

Supreme, at will to fow his well-fenc'd glebe,

With grain fucceffive; or with juicy herbs,

To fwell his milky kine; or feed, at eafe,

His flock in paftures warm.   His blazing hearth,

With copious fewel heap'd, defies the cold;

3   And

And houfewife-arts or teize the tangled wool,

Or, from the diftaff's hoard, the ductile thread,

With fportive hand entice; while to the wheel

The fprightly carol join'd, or plaintive fong

Diffufe, and artlefs fooths th' untutor'd ear,

With heart-felt ftrains, and the flow tafk beguiles.

    Nor hath the fun, with lefs propitious ray,

Shone on the mafters of the various fcene.

Witnefs the fplendid train! illuftrious names,

That claim precedence on the lifts of fame,

Nor fear oblivious time! enraptur'd Bards!

Or learned Sages! gracing, with their fame,

Their native foil, and my afpiring verfe.

    Say, now my dear companions! for enough

Of leifure to defcriptive fong is giv'n;

Say, fhall we, ere we part, with moral eye,

The fcene review, and the gay profpect clofe

With obfervation grave, as fober eve

Haftes now to wrap in fhades the clofing day?

Perhaps the moral ftrain delights you not!

Perhaps you blame the Mufe's quick retreat;

Intent to wander ftill along the plain,

In

In coverts cool, lull'd by the murm'ring ftream,

Or gentle breeze ; while playful fancy fkims,

With carelefs wing, the furfaces of things :

For deep refearch too indolent, too light

For grave reflection.   So the Syren queen

Tempted ALCIDES, on a flow'ry plain,

With am'rous blandifhment, and urg'd to wafte

His prime inglorious : but fair VIRTUE's form

Refcued the yielding youth, and fir'd his breaft

To manly toil, and glory's well-earn'd prize.

O ! in that dang'rous feafon, O ! beware

Of Vice, envenom'd weed ! and plant betimes

The feeds of virtue in th' untainted heart.

So on its fruit th' enraptur'd mind fhall feaft

When, to the fmiling day, and mirthful fcene

Night's folemn gloom, cold winter's chilling blafts,

And pain, and ficknefs, and old age fucceed.

Nor flight your faithful guide, my gentle train !

But, with a curious eye, expatiate free

O'er Nature's moral plan.   Tho' dark the theme,

Tho' formidable to the fenfual mind ;

Yet fhall the Mufe, with no fictitious aid,

Infpir'd, ftill guide you with her friendly voice,

And to each feeming ill fome greater good

Oppofe, and calm your lab'ring thoughts to reft.

   Nature herfelf bids us be ferious,

Bids us be wife ; and all her works rebuke

The ever-thoughtlefs, ever-titt'ring tribe.

What, tho' her lovely hills, and valleys fmile

To-day, in beauty dreft ? yet, ere three moons

Renew their orb, and to their wane decline,

Ere then the beauteous landfcape all will fade ;

The genial airs retire ; and fhiv'ring fwains

Shall, from the whiten'd plain, and driving ftorm,

Avert the fmarting cheek, and humid eye.

   So fome fair maid to time's devouring rage

Her bloom refigns, and, with a faded look,

Difgufts her paramour; unlefs thy charms,

O Virtue ! with more lafting beauty grace

Her lovelier mind, and, thro' declining age,

Fair deeds of piety, and modeft worth,

Still flourifh, and endear her ftill the more.

   Nor always lafts the Landfcape's gay attire

Till furly Winter, with his ruffian blafts,

Benumbs

Benumbs her tribes, and diſſipates her charms.

As ſickneſs oft the virgin's early bloom

Spoils immature, preventing hoary age,

So blaſts and mildews oft invade the fields

In all their beauty, and their ſummer's pride.

And oft the ſudden ſhow'r, or ſweeping * ſtorm

O'erflows the meads, and to the miry glebe

Lays cloſe the matted grain; with awful peal,

While the loud thunder ſhakes a guilty world,

And forked lightnings cleave the ſultry ſkies.

 Nor does the verdant mead, or bearded field

Alone the rage of angry ſkies ſuſtain.

Oft-times their influence dire the bleating flock,

Or lowing herd aſſails, and mocks the force

Of coſtly med'cine, or attendant care.

Such late the wrathful peſtilence, that ſeiz'd

In paſtures far retir'd, or guarded ſtalls,

* " Sæpe etiam immenſum cælo venit agmen aquarum,
 " Et fædam glomerant tempeſtatem imbribus atris
 " Collectæ ex alto nubes; ruit arduus æther,
 " Et pluviâ ingenti ſata læta, boumque labores
 " Diluit."   Virg.

          The

The dew-lap'd race I with plaintive lowings they,

And heavy eyes, confefs'd the pois'nous gale,

And drank infeǎion in each breath they drew.

Quick thro' their veins the burning fever ran,

And from their noftrils ftream'd the putrid rheum

Malignant; o'er their limbs faint languors crept,

And ftupefaǎion all their fenfes bound.

In vain their mafter, with officious hand,

From the pil'd mow the fweeteft lock prefents;

Or anxioufly prepares the tepid draught

Balfamic; they tbe proffer'd dainty loath,

And * Death exulting claims his deftin'd prey.

 Nor feldom † coughs, and watry rheums afflict

The woolly tribes, and on their vitals feize;

Thinning their folds; and, with their mangled limbs,

---

* " Hinc lætis vituli vulgo moriuntur in herbis,
 " Et dulces animas plena ad præfepia reddunt."
           Virg.

† " Non tam creber agens hyemem ruit æthere turbo,
 " Quam multæ pecudum peftes, nec fingula morbi
 " Corpora corripiunt, fed tota æftiva repentè
 " Spemque, gregemque fimul, cunǎamque ab origine
  " gentem."   Virg.

               And

And tatter'd fleeces, the averted eye

Difgufting; as the fqueamifh traveller,

With long-fufpended breath, hies o'er the plain.

And is their lord, proud Man! more fafe than they?

More privileg'd from the deftroying breath,

That, thro' the fecret fhade, in darknefs walks,

Or fmites whole paftures at the noon of day?

Ah! no, Death mark'd him from his infant birth;

Mark'd for his own, and, with envenom'd touch,

His vital blood defil'd.   Thro' all his veins

The fubtle poifon creeps; compounded joins

Its kindred mafs to his increafing bulk;

And, to the rage of angry elements,

Betrays his victim, poor, ill-fated Man;

Not furer born to live, than born to die!

In what a fad variety of forms

Clothes he his meffengers? Deliriums wild!

Inflated dropfy! flow confuming cough!

Jaundice, and gout, and ftone; convulfive fpafms;

The fhaking head, and the contracted limb;

And ling'ring atrophy, and hoary age;

And fecond childhood, flack'ning ev'ry nerve,

To

To joy, to reafon, and to duty dead!

I know thee, who thou art, offspring of Sin,

And Satan! nurs'd in Hell, and then let loofe

To range, with thy accurfed train, on earth,

When man, apoftate man! by Satan's wiles,

From life, from blifs, from God, and goodhefs fell!

Who knows thee not? who feels thee not within,

Plucking his heart-ftrings? whom haft thou not
        robb'd

Of parent, wife, or friend, as thou haft me?

Glutting the grave with ever-crowding guefts,

And, with their image, fad'ning ev'ry fcene,

Lefs peopled with the living than the dead!

   Thro' populous ftreets the never-ceafing bell

Proclaims, with folemn found, the parting breath;

Nor feldom from the village-tow'r is heard

The mournful knell.   Alike the graffy ridge,

With ofiers bound, and vaulted catacomb,

His fpoils inclofe.   Alike the fimple ftone,

And maufoleum proud, his pow'r atteft,

In wretched doggrel, or elab'rate verfe.

Perhaps

Perhaps the peasant's humble obsequies;
The flowing sheet, and pall of rusty hue,
Alarm you not.   You slight the simple throng;
And for the nodding plumes, and scutcheon'd hearse,
Your tears reserve.   Then mark, o'er yonder plain,
The grand procession suited to your taste.
I mock you not.   The sable pursuivants
Proclaim th' approaching state. Lo! now the plumes!
The nodding plumes, and scutcheon'd hearse ap-
    pear!
And clad in mournful weeds, a long sad train
Of slowly-moving pomp, that waits on death!
Nay—yet another melancholy train!
Another triumph of the ghastly fiend
Succeeds! 'Tis so.   Perhaps ye have not heard
The mournful tale.   Perhaps no messenger
Hath warn'd you to attend the solemn deed!
Then from the Muse the piteous story learn;
And, with her, on the grave procession wait,
That to their early tomb, to mould'ring dust
Of ancestors, that crowd the scanty vault,

                         Near

Near which our fong began, * Northampton bears,

The gay Northampton, and his beauteous † Bride!

Far other pageants in his youthful breaft

He cherifh'd, while, with delegated truft,

On ftately ceremonials, to the fhore;

Where Adria's waves the fea-girt city lave,

He went; and, with him, join'd in recent love,

His blooming Bride, of Beaufort's royal line,

The charming Somerset! But royal blood,

Nor youth, nor beauty, nor employment high,

Cou'd grant protection from the rude affault

Of that barbarian Death; who, without form,

To courts and cottages unbidden comes;

And his unwelcome embaffy fulfils,

Without diftinction, to the lofty peer,

The graceful bride, or peafant's homely race,

Ere, from her native foil, fhe faw the fun

---

* The Right Hon. the Earl of Northampton, who died on his return from an embaffy to Venice, while the Author was writing this poem.

† The Right Hon. the Countefs of Northampton, daughter to the Duke of Beaufort.

K   Run

Run half his annual courſe, in Latian climes,

She breath'd her laſt; him, ere that courſe was
    done,

Death met returning on the Gallic plains,

And ſent to join her yet unburied duſt:

Who, but this youthful pair's untimely fate

Muſt weep, who, but in theirs, may read their own?

    Another leſſon ſeek ye, other proof

Of vanity, and lamentable woe

Betiding man? Another ſcene to grace

With troops of victims the terrific king,

And humble wanton Folly's laughing ſons?

The Muſe ſhall from her faithful memory

A tale ſelect; a tale big with the fate

Of kings, and heroes on this now fair field

Embattled! but her ſong ſhall to your view

Their ranks embody, and, to future peace,

Their fierce deſigns, and hoſtile rage convert.

   Not on PHARSALIA's plain a *bolder ſtrife*

Was *held*, tho' twice with ROMAN blood diſtain'd,

Than when thy ſubjects, firſt imperial CHARLES!

Dared, in theſe fields, with arms their cauſe to plead.

                Where

* Where once the Romans pitch'd their hostile tents,

Other Campanias fair, and milder Alps

Exploring, now a nobler warrior stood,

His country's sov'reign liege ! Around his camp

A gallant train of loftiest rank attend,

By loyalty, and love of regal sway,

To mighty deeds impell'd.　Mean while below

Others no less intrepid courage boast,

From source as fair, the love of Liberty !

Dear Liberty ! when rightly understood,

Prime social bliss ! Oh ! may no fraud

Usurp thy name, to veil their dark designs

Of vile ambition, or licentious rage !

　Long time had they, with charge of mutual blame,

And fierce debate of speech, discordant minds

Avow'd, yet not to desp'rate chance of war

'Till now their cause referr'd : rude arbiter

Of fit, and right ! Unhappy native land !

Nought then avail'd that Nature form'd thy fields

So fair, and with her wat'ry barrier fenc'd !

　* A ROMAN camp at WARMINGTON, on the top of
EDGE-HILL.

K 2　　　　　　　　Nought

Nought then avail'd thy forms of guardian laws,

The work of ages, in a moment loft,

And ev'ry focial tie at once diffolv'd !

For now no more fweet peace, and order fair,

And kindred love remain'd, but hoftile rage

Inftead, and mutual jealoufy, and hate,

And tumult loud ! nor, hadft thou then been there,

* O TALBOT ! cou'd thy voice, fo often heard

On heav'nly themes ! nor † his fraternal ! fkill'd

In focial claims, the limits to define

Of law, and right, have calm'd the furious ftrife,

Or ftill'd the rattling thunder of the field.

Acrofs the plain, where the flight eminence,

And fcatter'd hedge-rows mark a midway fpace

To yonder ‡ town, once deem'd a royal court ;

Now harbouring no friends to royalty !

The popular troops their martial lines extend.

* The Rev. Mr. TALBOT, of KINETON.

† CH. HENRY TALBOT, Efq; of MARSTON, at the bottom of EDGE-HILL.

‡ KINETON, alias KINGTON. So called, as fome conjecture, from a caftle on a neighbouring hill, faid to have been a palace belonging to King JOHN.

High

High on the hill, the royal banners wave
Their faithful fignals.   Rang'd along the fteep,
The glitt'ring files, in burnifh'd armour clad,
Reflect the downward fun; and, with its gleam,
The diftant crowds affright, who trembling wait
For the dire onfet, and the dubious fight.

   As pent-up waters, fwell'd by fudden rains,
Their former bounds difdain, and foam, and rage
Impatient of reftraint; till, at fome breach,
Outward they burft impetuous, and mock
The peafant's feeble toil, which ftrives to check
Their headlong torrent; fo the royal troops,
With martial rage inflam'd, impatient wait
The trumpet's fummons.   At its fprightly call,
The airy feat they leave, and down the fteep,
Rank following rank, like wave fucceeding wave,
Rufh on the hoftile wings.   Dire was the fhock,
Dire was the clafh of arms!   The hoftile wings
Give way, and foon in flight their fafety feek.
They, with augmented force, and growing rage
The flying foe purfue.   But too fecure,
And counting of cheap conqueft quickly gain'd

O'er daftard minds, in wordy quarrels bold,

But flack by deeds to vindicate their claim,

In chace, and plunder long they wafte the day,

And late return, of order negligent.

Mean while the battle in the centre rag'd

With diff'rent fortune, by bold Essex led,

Experienc'd chief! and to the monarch's caufe,

And youthful race, for martial deeds unripe,

Menac'd deftruction.   In the royal breaft

High paffions rofe, by native dignity

Made more fublime, and urg'd to pow'rful act

By ftrong, * paternal love, and proud difdain

Of vulgar minds, arraigning in his race

The rights of fov'reignty, from ancient kings

In order fair deriv'd.   Amidft his troops

With hafte he flies, their broken ranks reforms,

To bold revenge re-animates their rage,

And from the foe his fhort-liv'd honour wrefts.

* Prince CHARLES, afterwards King CHARLES II. and
his brother the Duke of YoRK, afterwards King JAMES II.
were then in the field, the former being in the 13th, and the
latter juft enter'd into the 10th year of his age.

Now

Now Death, with hafty ftride, ftalks o'er the field,

Grimly exulting in the bloody fray.

Now on the crefted helm or burnifh'd fhield,

He ftamps new horrors; now the levell'd fword

With weightier force impells, with iron-hoof

Now tramples on th' expiring ranks; or gores

The foaming fteed againft th' oppofing fpear.

But chiefly on the cannon's brazen orb

He fits triumphant, and, with fatal aim,

Involves whole fquadrons in the fulph'rous ftorm.

Then * Lindsey fell, nor from the fhelt'ring ftraw,

Ceas'd he to plead his fov'reign's flighted caufe

Amidft furrounding foes; nor but with life,

Expir'd his loyalty.   His valiant fon †

Attempts his refcue, but attempts in vain !

Then ‡ Verney too, with many a gallant knight,

And faithful courtier, anxious for thy weal,

---

* Earl of Lindsey, the King's general.

† Lord Willoughby, fon to the Earl of Lindsey.

‡ Sir Edmund Verney, ftandard-bearer to the king.

K 4   Unhappy

Unhappy Prince! but mindlefs of their own,

Pour'd out his life upon the crimfon plain.

Then fell the gallant * Stewart, † Aubigny,

‡ And Kingsmill! He whofe monumental ftone

Protects his neighb'ring afhes, and his fame.

The clofing day compos'd the furious ftrife:

But for fhort time compos'd! anon to wake

With tenfold rage, and fpread a wider fcene

Of terror, and deftruction o'er the land!

Now mark the glories of the great debate!

Yon' grafs-green mount, where waves the planted
        pine,

And whifpers to the winds the mournful tale,

Contains them in its monumental mould;

A flaughter'd crew, promifcuous lodg'd below!

Still as the plowman breaks the clotted glebe,

He ever and anon fome trophy finds,

* Lord Stewart.

† Lord Aubigny, fon to the Duke of Lenox.

‡ Captain Kingsmill, buried at Radway; whofe monument fee at the end of the Poem.

The

The * relicks of the war—or rufty fpear,

Or canker'd ball ; but, from fepulchral foil,

Cautious he turns afide the fhining fteel,

Left haply, at its touch, uncover'd bones

Should ftart to view, and blaft his rural toil.

    Such were the fruits of Paffion, froward Will,

And unfubmitting Pride! Worfe ftorms than thofe

That rend the fky, and wafte our cultur'd fields!

Strangers alike to man's primæval ftate,

Ere Evil entrance found to this fair world,

Permitted, not ordain'd, whatever Pride

May dream of order in a world of fin,

Or pre-exiftent foul, and penal doom

For crimes unknown.   More wife, more happy he !

Who in his breaft oft pond'ring, and perplext

With endlefs doubt, and learning's fruitlefs toil,

His weary mind at length repofes fure

    * " Scilicet et tempus veniet, cum finibus illis,
     " Agricola incurvo terram molitus aratro,
     " Exefa inveniet fcabrâ rubigine pila,
     " Aut gravibus raftris galeas pulfabit inanes,
     " Grandiaque effoffis mirabitur offa fepulchris."

                                       VIRG.

                                       On

On Heav'n's attefted oracles.   To them

Submifs he bows, convinc'd, however weak

His reafon the myfterious plan to folve,

That all He wills is right, who, ere the worlds

Were form'd, in his all-comprehenfivė mind,

Saw all that was, or is, or e'er fhall be.

Who to whate'er exifts; or lives, or moves,

Throughout creation's wide extent, gave life,

Gave being, pow'r, and thought to act, to move

Impelling, or impell'd, to all ordain'd

Their ranks, relations, and dependencies,

And can direct, fufpend, controul their pow'rs,

Elfe were he not fupreme! Who bids the winds

Be ftill, and they obey ; who to the fea

Affigns its bounds, and calms its boifterous waves,

Who, with like eafe can moral difcord rule,

And all apparent evil turn to good.

    Hail then, ye fons of Eve! th' unerring guide,

The fovereign grant receive, fin's antidote!

A cure for all our griefs! So heav'nly Truth .

Shall wide difplay her captivating charms,

And Peace her dwelling fix with human race.

So Love thro' ev'ry clime his gentle reign
Shall fpread, and at his call difcordant realms
Shall beat their fwords to plowfhares, and their fpears
To pruning-hooks, nor more learn murth'rous war.
So when revolving years, by Heav'n's decree,
·Their circling courfe have run, new firmaments,
With bleffings fraught, fhall fill the bright expanfe,
Of tempefts void, and thunder's angry voice.
New verdure fhall arife to cloathe the fields :
New EDENS! teeming with immortal fruit!
No more the wing'd inhabitants of air
Or thofe that range the fields, or fkim the flood,
Their fiercenefs fhall retain, but brute with brute,
And all with man in amicable league
Shall join, and enmity for ever ceafe.

　　Remains there aught to crown the rapt'rous theme?
'Tis this, unfading joy, beyond the reach
Of elemental worlds, and fhort-liv'd time.
This too is yours—from outward fenfe conceal'd,
But, by refemblance of external things,
Inward difplay'd, to elevate the foul
To thoughts fublime, and point her way to Heav'n.

　　　　　　　　　　　　　　　　So,

So, from the top of NEBO's lofty mount,

The patriot-leader of JEHOVAH's fons

The promis'd land furvey'd; to CANAAN's race

A fplendid theatre of frantic joys,

And fatal mirth, beyond whofe fcanty bounds

Darknefs, and horror dwell! Emblem to *him*

Of fairer fields, and happier feats above!

Then clofed his eyes to mortal fcenes, to wake

In the bright regions of eternal day.

THE END.

LABOUR

LABOUR, and GENIUS:

OR, THE

Mill - Stream, *and the* Cafcade.

A F A B L E.

INSCRIBED TO

WILLIAM SHENSTONE, Esq.

—— " difcordia Semina rerum."
                                OVID.

LABOUR, AND GENIUS:

·OR, THE

Mill - Stream, *and the* Cafcade.

A   F A B L E.

NATURE, with lib'ral hand, difpenfes
　　　Her apparatus of the fenfes,
In articles of gen'ral ufe,
Nerves, finews, mufcles, bones profufe.
Diftinguifhing her fav'rite race
With form erect, and featur'd face:
The flowing hair, the polifh'd fkin—
But, for the furniture within,

Whether

Whether it be of brains, or lead,

What matters it, fo there's a head?

For wifeft noddle feldom goes,

But as 'tis led by corp'ral nofe.

Nor is it thinking much, but doing,

That keeps our tenements from ruin.

And hundreds eat, who fpin, or knit,

For one that lives by dint of wit.

   The fturdy threfher plies his flail,

And what to this doth wit avail?

Who learns from wit to prefs the fpade?

Or thinks 'twou'd mend the cobler's trade?

The pedlar, with his cumb'rous pack,

Carries his brains upon his back.

Some wear them in full-bottom'd wig,

Or hang them by with *queue*, or *pig*.

Reduc'd, till they return again,

In difhabille, to common men.

Then why, my friend, is wit fo rare?

That fudden flafh, that makes one ftare!

A meteor's blaze, a dazzling fhew!

Say what it is, for well you know.

       I   Or,

Or, if you can with patience hear
A witlefs Fable, lend an ear.

BETWIXT two floping verdant hills,
A Current pour'd its carelefs rills,
Which unambitious crept along,
With weeds, and matted grafs o'erhung.
Till *rural Genius*, on a day,
Chancing along its banks to ftray,
Remark'd with penetrating look
The latent merits of the Brook,
Much griev'd to fee fuch talents hid,
And thus the dull by-ftanders chid.

How blind is man's incurious race,
The fcope of Nature's plans to trace?
How do ye mangle half her charms,
And fright her hourly with alarms?
Disfigure now her fwelling mounds,
And now contract her fpacious bounds?
Fritter her faireft lawns to alleys,
Bare her green hills, and hide her valleys?

L.   Confine

Confine her ſtreams with rule and line,

And counteract her whole deſign?

Neglecting, where ſhe points the way,

Her eaſy dictates to obey?

To bring her hidden worth to ſight;

And place her charms in faireſt light?

 Alike to *intellectuals* blind,

'Tis thus you treat the youthful mind;

Miſtaking gravity for ſenſe,

For dawn of wit, impertinence.

 The boy of genuine parts, and merit,

For ſome unlucky prank of ſpirit,

With frantic rage is ſcourg'd from ſchool,

And branded with the name of fool,

Becauſe his active blood flow'd faſter

Than the dull puddle of his maſter.

While the ſlow plodder trots along,

Thro' thick and thin, thro' proſe and ſong,

Inſenſible of all their graces,

But learn'd in words, and common phraſes:

Till in due time he's mov'd to college,

To ripen theſe choice ſeeds of knowledge.

So fome tafte-pedant, wond'rous wife,

Exerts his genius in dirt-pies.

Delights the tonfile yew to raife,

But hates your laurels, and your bays,

Becaufe too rambling, and luxuriant,

Like forward youths, of brains too prurient.

Makes puns, and anagrams in box,

And turns his trees to bears, and cocks.

Excels in quaint jette-d'eau, or fountain,

Or leads his ftream acrofs a mountain,

To fhew its fhallownefs, and pride,

In a broad grin, on t'other fide.

Perverting all the rules of fenfe,

Which never offers violence,

But gently leads where Nature tends,

Sure, with applaufe, to gain its ends.

But one example may teach more,

Than precepts hackney'd o'er, and o'er.

Then mark this *Rill*, with weeds o'erhung,

Unnotic'd by the vulgar throng!

Ev'n this, conducted by my laws,

Shall rife to fame, attract applaufe;

L 2   Inftruct

Inftruct in * fable, fhine in fong,

And be the theme of ev'ry tongue.

He faid : and, to his fav'rite fon,

Confign'd the tafk, and will'd it done.

DAMON his counfel wifely weigh'd,

And carefully the fcene furvey'd.

And, tho' it feems he faid but little,

He took his meaning to a tittle.

And firft, his purpofe to befriend,

A bank he rais'd at th' upper end :

Compact, and clofe its outward fide,

To ftay, and fwell the gath'ring tide:

But, on its inner, rough and tall,

A ragged cliff, a rocky wall.

The channel next he op'd to view,

And, from its courfe, the rubbifh drew.

Enlarg'd it now, and now, with line

Oblique, purfued his fair defign.

* See Fable XLI. and LI. in DODSLEY's new-invented
Fables, and many little pieces printed in the public papers.

Preparing

Preparing here the mazy way,

And there the fall for fportive play.

The precipice abrupt, and fteep,

The pebbled road, and cavern deep.

The rooty feat, where beft to view

The fairy fcene, at diftance due.

He laft invok'd the Dryads aid,

And fring'd the borders round with fhade.

Tap'ftry, by Nature's fingers wove,

No mimic, but a real grove:

Part hiding, part admitting day,

The fcene to grace the future play.

DAMON perceives, with ravifh'd eyes,

The beautiful enchantment rife.

Sees fweetly blended fhade, and light,

Sees ev'ry part with each unite.

Sees each, as he directs, affume

A livelier dye, or deeper gloom:

So, fafhion'd by the painter's fkill,

New forms the glowing canvas fill.

So, to the fummer's fun, the rofe,

And jeffamin their charms difclofe,

L 3   While,

While, all intent on this retreat,

He faw his fav'rite work compleat,

Divine enthufiafm feiz'd his breaft,

And thus his tranfport he exprefs'd.

" Let others toil, for wealth, or pow'r,

I court the fweetly-vacant hour :

Down life's fmooth current calmly glide,

Nor vex'd with cares, nor rack'd with pride.

Give me, O Nature ! to explore

Thy lovely charms, I afk no more.

For thee I fly from vulgar eyes,

For thee I vulgar cares defpife.

For thee Ambition's charms refign ;

Accept a vot'ry, wholly thine.

Yet ftill let Friendfhip's joys be near,

Still, on thefe plains, her train appear.

By Learning's fons my haunts be trod,

And STAMFORD's feet imprint my fod.

For STAMFORD oft hath deign'd to ftray

Around my Leafow's flow'ry way.

And, where his honour'd fteps have rov'd,

Oft have his gifts thofe fcenes improv'd.

To him I'll dedicate my cell,

To him fufpend the votive fpell.

His name fhall heighten ev'ry charm,

His name protect my groves from harm,

Protect my harmlefs fport from blame,

And turn obfcurity to fame."

He fpake. His hand the pencil guides,

And * STAMFORD o'er the fcene prefides.

The proud device, with borrow'd grace,

Conferr'd new luftre on the place :

As books, by dint of dedication,

Enjoy their patron's reputation.

Now, launching from its lofty fhore,

The loofen'd ftream began to roar :

As headlong, from the rocky mound,

It rufh'd into the vaft profound.

There checkt awhile, again it flow'd

Glitt'ring along the channel'd road :

* The fcene here referr'd to, was infcribed to the Right
Hon. the Earl of STAMFORD; but fince to WILLIAM
SHENSTONE, Efq.

From

From steep to steep, a frequent fall,

Each diff'rent, and each natural.

Obstructing roots and rocks between,

Diversify th' enchanted scene;

While winding now, and intricate,

Now more develop'd, and in state,

Th' united Stream, with rapid force,

Pursues amain its downward course,

Till at your feet absorb'd, it hides

Beneath the ground its bustling tides.

　　With prancing steeds, and liv'ried trains,

Soon daily shone the bord'ring plains.

And distant sounds foretold th' approach

Of frequent chaise, and crowded coach.

For sons of Taste, and daughters fair,

Hasted the sweet surprize to share:

While * HAGLEY wonder'd at their stay,

And hardly brook'd the long delay.

　　Not distant far below, a Mill

Was built upon a neighb'ring Rill:

* The seat of the Right Hon. Lord LYTTELTON, distant but a few miles from the Leasows.

Whose

Whofe pent-up ftream, whene'er let loofe,

Impell'd a wheel, clofe at its fluice,

So ftrongly, that, by friction's pow'r,

'Twou'd grind the firmeft grain to flow'r.

Or, by a correfpondence new,

With hammers, and their clatt'ring crew,

Wou'd fo beftir her active ftumps,

On iron-blocks, tho' arrant lumps,

That, in a trice, fhe'd manage matters,

To make 'em all as fmooth as platters.

Or flit a bar to rods quite taper,

With as much eafe, as you'd cut paper.

For, tho' the lever gave the blow,

Yet it was lifted from below;

And wou'd for ever have lain ftill,

But for the buftling of the Rill;

Who, from her ftately pool, or ocean,

Put all the weels, and logs in motion;

Things in their nature very quiet,

Tho' making all this noife, and riot.

    This Stream, that cou'd in toil excel,

Began with foolifh pride to fwell:

Piqu'd

Piqu'd at her neighbour's reputation,
And thus exprefs'd her indignation.

" Madam ! methinks you're vaftly proud,
You was'nt us'd to talk fo loud.

Nor cut fuch capers in your pace,
Marry ! what anticks, what grimace !

For fhame ! don't give yourfelf fuch airs,
In flaunting down thofe hideous ftairs.

Nor put yourfelf in fuch a flutter,
Whate'er you do, you dirty gutter !

I'd have you know, you upftart minx !
Ere you were form'd, with all your finks,

A Lake I was, compar'd with which,
Your Stream is but a paltry Ditch :

And ftill, on honeft Labour bent,
I ne'er a fingle *flafh* mifpent.

And yet no folks of high degree,
Wou'd e'er vouchfafe to vifit me,

As, in their coaches, by they rattle,
Forfooth ! to hear your idle prattle.

Tho' half the bufinefs of my flooding
Is to provide them cakes, and pudding :

Or

Or furnifh ftuff for many a trinket,

Which, tho' fo fine, you fcarce wou'd think it,

When * BOULTON's fkill has fix'd their beauty,

To my rough toil firft ow'd their duty.

But I'm plain *Goody* of the Mill ;

And you are—*Madam Cafcadille !*"

   " Dear Coz, reply'd the beauteous Torrent,

Pray do not difcompofe your current.

That we all from one fountain flow,

Hath been agreed on long ago.

Varying our talents, and our tides,

As chance, or education guides.

That I have either note, or name,

I owe to Him who gives me fame.

Who teaches all our kind to flow,

Or gaily fwift, or gravely flow.

Now in the lake, with glaffy face,

Now moving light, with dimpled grace.

Now gleaming from the rocky height, .

Now, in rough eddies, foaming white.

* An eminent merchant, and very ingenious mechanic, at
the So-ho Manufactory, near BIRMINGHAM.

                                            Nor

Nor envy me the gay, or great,

That vifit my obfcure retreat.

None wonders that a clown can dig,

But 'tis fome art to dance a jig.

Your talents are employ'd for ufe,

Mine to give pleafure, and amufe.

And tho', dear Coz, no folks of tafte

Their idle hours with you will wafte,

Yet many a grift comes to your mill,

Which helps your mafter's bags to fill.

While I, with all my notes, and trilling,

For DAMON never got a fhilling.

Then, gentle Coz, forbear your clamours,

Enjoy your hoppers, and your hammers:

We gain our ends by diff'rent ways,

And you get Bread, and I get—Praife.

MISCELLANEOUS PIECES.

MISCELLANEOUS PIECES.

A R D E N N A.

A PASTORAL-ECLOGUE.

To a LADY.

DAMON, and LYCIDAS.

WHEN o'er the Weſtern world fair Science
   ſpread
Her genial ray, and Gothic darkneſs fled,
To BRITAIN's Iſle the Muſes took their way,
And taught her liſt'ning groves the tuneful lay.
'Twas then two Swains the Doric reed eſſay'd
To ſing the praiſes of a peerleſs maid.
On ARDEN's bliſsful plain her ſeat ſhe choſe,
And hence her rural name ARDENNA roſe.

       In

In fportive verfe alternately they vied,

Thus DAMON fang, and LYCIDAS replied.

DAMON.

Here, gentle Swain, beneath the fhade reclin'd,

Remit thy labours, and unbend thy mind.

Well with the fhepherd's ftate our cares agree,

For Nature prompts to pleafing induftry.

'Tis this to all her gifts frefh beauty yields,

Health to our flocks, and plenty to our fields.

Yet hath fhe not impos'd unceafing toil,

Not reftlefs plowfhares always vex the foil.

Then, Shepherd, take the bleffings Heav'n beftows,

Affift the fong, and fweeten our repofe.

LYCIDAS.

While others, funk in fleep, or live in vain,

Or, flaves of indolence, but wake to pain,

Me let the call of earlieft birds invite

To hail th' approaches of returning light;

To tafte the frefhnefs of the chearful morn,

While glift'ring dew-drops hang on ev'ry thorn.

Hence

Hence all the blifs that centers in our kind,

Health to the blood, and vigour to the mind.

Hence ev'ry tafk its meet attendance gains,

And leifure hence to liften to thy ftrains.

DAMON.

Thrice happy fwain, fo fitly form'd to fhare

The fhepherd's labour, and ARDENNA's care!

To tell ARDENNA's praife the rural train

Infcribe the verfe, or chant ít o'er the plain.

Plains, hills, and woods return the well-known found,

And the fmooth beech records the fportive wound.

Then, LYCIDAS, let us the chorus join,

So bright a theme our mufic fhall refine.

Efcap'd from all the bufy world admires,

Hither the philofophic dame retires;

For in the bufy world, or poets feign,

Intemp'rate vice, and giddy pleafures reign;

Then, when from crowds the Loves, and Graces flew,

To thefe lone fhades the beauteous maid withdrew,

To ftudy Nature in this calm retreat,

And with confed'rate Art her charms compleat.

M   How

How fweet their union is, ye fhepherds, fay,
And thou who form'dft the reed infpire my lay.

Her praife I fing by whom our flocks are freed
From the rough bramble, and envenom'd weed;
Who to green paftures turns the dreary wafte,
With fcatter'd woods in carelefs beauty grac'd.

'Tis fhe, ARDENNA ! Guardian of the fcene,
Who bids the mount to fwell, who fmooths the green,
Who drains the marfh, and frees the ftruggling flood
From its divided rule, and ftrife with mud.
She winds its courfe the copious ftream to fhew,
And fhe in fwifter currents bids it flow;
Now fmoothly gliding with an even pace,
Now dimpling o'er the ftones with roughen'd grace:
With glaffy furface now ferenely bright,
Now foaming from the rock all filver white.

'Tis fhe the rifing bank with beeches crowns,
Now fpreads the fcene, and now contracts its bounds.
Cloaths the bleak hill with verdure ever gay,
And bids our feet thro' myrtle-valleys ftray.
She for her fhepherds rears the rooty fhed,
The checquer'd pavement, and the ftraw-wove bed.

For

For them fhe fcoops the grotto's cool retreat,

From ftorms a fhelter, and a fhade in heat.

Directs their hands the verdant arch to bend,

And with the leafy roof its gloom extend.

Shells, flint, and ore their mingled graces join,

And rocky fragments aid the chafte defign.

LYCIDAS.

Hail happy lawns! where'er we turn our eyes,

Frefh beauties bloom, and opening wonders rife.

Whileome thefe charming fcenes with grief I view'd

A barren wafte, a dreary folitude!

My drooping flocks their ruffet paftures mourn'd,

And lowing herds the plaintive moan return'd.

With weary feet from field to field they ftray'd,

Nor found their hunger's painful fenfe allay'd.

But now no more a dreary fcene appears,

No more its prickly boughs the bramble rears,

No more my flocks lament th' unfruitful foil,

Nor mourn their ragged fleece, or fruitlefs toil.

M 2   DAMON.

DAMON.

As this fair lawn excels the ruſhy mead,
As firs the thorn, and flow'rs the pois'nous weed,
Far as the warbling ſky-larks ſoar on high,
Above the clumſy bat, or buzzing fly;
So matchleſs moves ARDENNA o'er the green,
In mind alike excelling as in mien.

LYCIDAS.

Sweet is the fragrance of the damaſk roſe,
And bright the dye that on its ſurface glows,
Fair is the poplar riſing on the plain,
Of ſhapely trunk, and lofty branches vain;
But neither ſweet the roſe, nor bright its dye,
Nor poplar fair, if with her charms they vie.

DAMON.

Grateful is ſunſhine to the ſportive lambs,
The balmy dews delight the nibbling dams;
But kindlier warmth ARDENNA's ſmiles impart,
A balm more rich her leſſons to the heart.

LYCIDAS.

LYCIDAS.

No more POMONA's guiding hand we need,
Nor FLORA's help to paint th' enamell'd mead,
Nor CERES' care to guard the rifing grain,
And fpread the yellow plenty o'er the plain;
ARDENNA's precepts ev'ry want fupply,
The grateful lay what fhepherd can deny?

DAMON.

A theme fo pleafing, with the day begun,
Too foon were ended with the fetting fun.
But fee o'er yonder hill the parting ray,
And hark! our bleating flocks reprove our ftay.

M 3   THE

The SCAVENGERS.

A TOWN-ECLOGUE.

" Dulcis odor lucri ox re quâlibet."

A WAKE, my Mufe, prepare a loftier theme.
  The winding valley, and the dimpled ftreani
Delight not all : quit, quit the verdant field,
And try what dufty ftreets, and alleys yield.

 Where Avón wider flows, and gathers fame,
Stands a fair town, and WARWICK is its name.
For ufeful arts entitled once to fhare
The gentle ETHELFLEDA's guardian care.
Nor lefs for deeds of chivalry renown'd,
When her own GUY was with her laurels crown'd.
Now Syren Sloth holds here her tranquil reign,
And binds in filken bonds the feeble train.
No frowning knights in uncouth armour lac'd,
Seek now for monfters on the dreary wafte :
In thefe foft fcenes they chace a gentler prey,
No monfters ! but as dangerous as they.

In

In diff'rent forms as fure deftruction lies,

They have no claws 'tis true—but they have eyes.

Laft of the toiling race there liv'd a pair,

Bred up in labour, and inur'd to care!

To fweep the ftreets their tafk from fun to fun,

And feek the naftinefs which others fhun.

More plodding wight, or dame you ne'er fhall fee,

He Gaffer Pestel hight, and Gammer fhe.

As at their door they fate one fummer's day,

Old Pestel firft effay'd the plaintive lay:

His gentle mate the plaintive lay return'd,

And thus alternately their cares they mourn'd.

Old Pestel.

Alas! was ever fuch fine weather feen,

How dufty are the roads, the ftreets how clean!

How long, ye Almanacks! will it be dry?

Empty my cart how long, and idle I!

Ev'n at the beft the times are not fo good,

But 'tis hard work to fcrape a livelihood.

The cattle in the ftalls refign their life,

And baulk the fhambles, and th' unbloody knife.

While

While farmers fit at home in penfive gloom,
And turnpikes threaten to compleat my doom.

WIFE.

Well! for the turnpike that will do no hurt,
Some fay the managers are friends to dirt.
But much I fear this murrain where 'twill end,
For fure the cattle did our door befriend.
Oft have I hail'd 'em, as they ftalk'd along,
Their fat the butchers pleas'd, but me their dung.

OLD PESTEL.

See what a little dab of dirt is here!
But yields all WARWICK more, O tell me where? -
Yet, on this fpot, tho' now fo naked feen,
Heaps upon heaps, and loads on loads have been.
Bigger, and bigger, the proud dunghill grew,
Till my diminifh'd houfe was hid from view.

WIFE.

Ah! Gaffer PESTEL, what brave days were thofe,
When higher than our houfe our muckhill rofe!

The

The growing mount I view'd with joyful eyes,

And mark'd what each load added to its fize.

Wrapt in its fragrant fteam we often fate,

And to its praifes held delightful chat.

Nor did I e'er neglect my mite to pay,

To fwell the goodly heap from day to day.

A cabbage once I bought ; but fmall the coft—

Nor do I think the farthing all was loft.

Again you fold its well-digefted ftore,

To dung the garden where it grew before.

OLD PESTEL.

What tho' the beaus, and powder'd coxcombs jeer'd,

And at the fcavenger's employment fneer'd,

Yet then at night content I told my gains,

And thought well paid their malice, and my pains.

Why toils the tradefman, but to fwell his ftore ?

Why craves the wealthy landlord ftill for more ?

Why will our gentry flatter, fawn, and lie ?

Why pack the cards, and what d'ye call't—the die ?

All, all the pleafing paths of gain purfue,

And wade thro' thick, and thin, as we folks do.

Sweet

Sweet is the scent that from advantage springs,
And nothing dirty which good int'reft brings.

WIFE.

When goody DOBBINS call'd me nafty bear,
And talk'd of kennels, and the ducking-chair,
With patience I cou'd hear the fcolding quean,
For fure 'twas dirtinefs that kept me clean.
Clean was my gown on Sundays, if not fine,
Nor Mrs. ————'s cap fo white as mine.
A flut in filk, or kerfey is the fame,
Nor fweeteft always is the fineft dame.

Thus wail'd they pleafure paft, and prefent cares,
While the ftarv'd hog join'd his complaint with theirs.
To ftill his grunting diff'rent ways they tend,
To * WEST-STREET he, and fhe to * COTTON-END.

* Names of the moft remote, and oppofite parts of the
Town.

ABSENCE.

A B S E N C E.

WITH leaden foot Time creeps along
    While DELIA is away,
With her, nor plaintive was the fong,
    Nor tedious was the day.

Ah! envious pow'r! reverfe my doom,
    Now double thy career,
Strain ev'ry nerve, ftretch ev'ry plume,
    And reft them when fhe's here.

To A L A D Y.

WHEN Nature joins a beauteous face
    With fhape, and air, and life, and grace,
To ev'ry imperfection blind,
I fpy no blemifh in the mind.

When

When wit flows pure from STELLA's tongue,
Or animates the fprightly fong,
Our hearts confefs the pow'r divine,
Nor lightly prize its mortal fhrine.

Good-nature will a conqueft gain,
Tho' wit, and beauty figh in vain.

When gen'rous thoughts the breaft infpire,
I wifh its rank, and fortunes higher.

When SIDNEY's charms again unite
To win the foul, and blefs the fight,
Fair, and learn'd, and good, and great!
An earthly goddefs is compleat.

But when I fee a fordid mind
With affluence, and ill-nature join'd,
And pride without a grain of fenfe,
And without beauty infolence,
The creature with contempt I view,
And fure 'tis like Mifs———you know who.

To

To a LADY working a Pair of RUFFLES.

WHAT means this ufelefs coft, this wanton
  pride?
To purchafe fopp'ry from yon' foreign ftrand!
To fpurn our native ftores, and arts afide,
  And drain the riches of a needy land!

Pleas'd I furvey, fair nymph, your happy fkill,
  Yet view it by no vulgar critic's laws:
With nobler aim I draw my fober quill,
  Anxious to lift each art in Virtue's caufe.

Go on, dear maid, your utmoft pow'r effay,
  And if for fame your little bofom heave,
Know patriot-*bands* your merit fhall difplay,
  And amply pay the graces they receive.

Let ev'ry nymph like you the gift prepare,
  And banifh foreign pomp, and coftly fhow;
What lover but wou'd burn the prize to wear,
  Or blufh by you pronounc'd his country's foe?

                                        Your

Your fmiles can win when patriot-fpeeches fail,

　　Your frowns controul when juftice threats in vain,

O'er ftubborn minds your foftnefs can prevail,

　　And placemen drop the bribe if you complain.

Then rife the guardians of your country's fame,

　　Or wherefore were ye form'd like angels fair?

By beauty's force our venal hearts reclaim,

　　And fave the drooping Virtues from defpair.

FEMALE EMPIRE.

A TRUE HISTORY.

LIKE Bruin's was AVARO's breaft,

　　No foftnefs harbour'd there ;

While SYLVIO fome concern exprefs'd,

　　When beauty fhed a tear.

In HYMEN's bands they both were tied,

　　As * CUPID's archives fhew ye ;

Proud CELIA was AVARO's bride,

　　And SYLVIO's gentle CHLOE.

　　　　* The parifh-regifter.

　　　　　　　　　　　　　　Like

Like other nymphs, at church they fwore,
　To honour, and obey, 　 .
Which, with each learned nymph before,
　They foon explain'd away.

If CHLOE now wou'd have her will,
　Her ftreaming eyes prevail'd,
Or if her fwain prov'd cruel ftill,
　Hyfterics never fail'd.

But CELIA fcorn'd the plaintive moan,
　And heart-diffolving fhow'r;
With flafhing eye, and angry tone,
　She beft maintain'd her pow'r.

Yet once the mandates of his Turk
　AVARO durft refufe;
For why? important was his work,
　" To regifter old fhoes !"

And does, faid fhe, the wretch difpute
　My claim fuch clowns to rule?
If CELIA cannot charm a brute,
　She can chaftife a fool.

Then

Then ſtrait ſhe to his cloſet flew,

His private thoughts ſhe tore,

And from its place the poker drew,

That fell'd him on the floor.

Henceforth, ſaid ſhe, my calls regard,

Own mine the ſtronger plea,

Nor let thy vulgar cares retard

The female rites of tea.

Victorious ſex! alike your art,

And puiſſance we dread ;

For if you cannot break our heart,

'Tis plain you'll break our head.

Place me, ye Gods, beneath the throne

Which gentle ſmiles environ,

And I'll ſubmiſſion gladly own,

Without a rod of iron.

On Mr. Samuel Cooke's POEMS.

WRITTEN IN THE YEAR 1749.

INDEED, Mafter Cooke !
   You have made fuch a book,
As the learned in paftry admire :
   But other wits joke
   To fee fuch a fmoke
Without any vifible fire.

   What a nice bill of fare,
   Of whatever is rare,
And approv'd by the critics of tafte !
   Not a claffical bit,
   Ev'ry fancy to hit,
But here in due order is plac'd.

N   Yet,

Yet, for all this parade,

You are but a dull blade,

And your lines are all fcragged, and raw ;

And tho' you've hack'd, and have hew'd,

And have fqueez'd, and have ftew'd,

Your forc'd-meat isn't all worth a ftraw.

Tho' your fatire you fpit,

'Tisn't feafon'd a bit,

And your puffs are as heavy as lead ;

Call each difh what you will,

Boil, roaft, hafh, or grill,

Yet ftill it is all a calve's-head.

I don't mind your huffing,

For you've put fuch vile ftuff in,

I proteft I'm as fick as a dog ;

Were you leaner, or fatter,

I'd not mince the matter,

You're not fit to drefs Æsop a frog.

Then

Then, good mafter Slice!
Shut up fhop, if your wife,
And th' unwary no longer trepan;
Such advice indeed is hard,
And may ftick in your gizzard,
But digeft it as well as you can.

THE MISTAKE.

ON CAPTAIN BLUFF. 1750.

SAYS a Gofling, almoft frighten'd out of her wits,
   Help mother, or elfe I fhall go into fits.
I have had fuch a fright, I fhall never recover,
O! that *Hawke*, that you've told us of over and
    over.
See, there, where he fits, with his terrible face,
And his coat how it glitters all over with lace.
With his fharp hooked nofe, and his fword at his heel,
How my heart it goes pit-a-pat, pray, mother, feel.

         Says

Says the Goofe, very gravely, Pray don't talk fo wild,

Thofe looks are as harmlefs as mine are, my child.

And as for his fword there, fo bright, and fo nice,

I'll be fworn 'twill hurt nothing befides frogs, and mice.

Nay, prithee don't hang fo about me, let loofe,

I tell thee he dares not fay—bo to a Goofe.

In fhort there is not a more innocent fowl,

Why, inftead of a *Hawke*, look ye, child, 'tis an *Owl*.

To a LADY,

WITH A BASKET OF FRUIT,

ONCE of forbidden fruit the mortal tafte
    Chang'd beauteous EDEN to a dreary wafte.

Here you may freely eat, fecure the while

From latent poifon, or infidious guile.

Yet O! cou'd I but happily infufe

Some fecret charm into the fav'ry juice,

Of pow'r to tempt your gentle breaft to fhare

With me the peaceful cot, and rural fare:

A diff'rent fate fhou'd crown the bleft device,

And change my Defart to a Paradife.

PEYTOE's

*PEYTOE's GHOST.

TO CRAVEN's health, and social joy,
 The festive night was kept,
While mirth and patriot spirit flow'd,
 And Dullness only slept.

When from the jovial crowd I stole,
 And homeward shap'd my way ;
And pass'd along by CHESTERTON,
 All at the close of day.

The sky with clouds was over-cast :
 An hollow tempest blow'd,
And rains and foaming cataracts
 Had delug'd all the road.

When thro' the dark and lonesome shade,
 Shone forth a sudden light ;
And soon distinct an human form,
 Engag'd my wondering sight.

* Was the late Lord WILLOUGHBY DE BROKE.

  Onward

Onward it mov'd with graceful port,
  And foon o'ertook my fpeed;
Then thrice I lifted up my hands,
  And thrice I check'd my fteed.

Who art thou, paffenger, it cry'd,
  From yonder mirth retir'd?
That here purfu'ft thy cheerlefs way,
  Benighted, and be-mir'd.

I am, faid I, a country clerk,
  A clerk of low degree,
And yonder gay and gallant fcene,
  Suits not a curacy.

But I have feen fuch fights to-day,
  As make my heart full glad,
Altho' it is but dark, 'tis true,
  And eke—my road is bad.

For I have feen lords, knights, and fquires,
  Of great and high renown,
To chufe a knight for this fair fhire,
  All met at WARWICK Town.

A wight

A wight of skill to ken our laws,
    Of courage to defend,
Of worth to serve the public cause,
    Before a private end.

And such they found, if right I guess—
    Of gentle blood he came;
Of morals firm, of manners mild,
    And * CRAVEN is his name.

Did half the British tribunes share
    Experienc'd † MORDAUNT's truth,
Another half, like CRAVEN, boast
    A free unbiass'd youth:

The sun I trow, in all his race,
    No happier realm should find;
Nor BRITONS hope for aught in vain,
    From warmth with prudence join'd.

* Hon. WILLIAM CRAVEN, of WYKIN; he was afterwards Lord CRAVEN.

† The late Sir CHARLES MORDAUNT, Bart.

"Go

"Go on, my Country, favour'd foil,
  Such Patriots to produce!
Go on, my Countrymen, he cry'd,
  Such Patriots ftill to chufe."

This faid, the placid form retir'd,
  Behind the veil of night;
Yet bade me, for my Country's good,
  The folemn tale recite.

To a LADY,

Furnishing her LIBRARY, at ****, in WARWICKSHIRE.

WHEN juft proportion in each part,
  And colours mixt with niceft art,
Confpire to fhew the grace and mien
Of CLOE, or the CYPRIAN Queen:
With elegance throughout refin'd,
That fpeaks the paffions of the mind,

The

The glowing canvas will proclaim,

A RAPHAEL's, or a TITIAN's name.

So where thro' ev'ry learned page,

Each diftant clime, each diftant age

Difplay a rich variety,

Of wifdom in epitome;

Such elegance and tafte will tell

The hand, that could feleét fo well.

But when we all their beauties view,

United and improv'd by You,

We needs muft own an emblem faint,

T' exprefs thofe charms no art can paint.

Books muft, with fuch correétnefs writ,

Refine another's tafte and wit;

'Tis to your merit only due,

That theirs can be refin'd by You.

To

To WILLIAM SHENSTONE, Esq.

ON RECEIVING A GILT POCKET-BOOK. 1751.

THESE spotless leaves, this neat array,
    Might *well* invite your charming quill,
In fair assemblage to display
    The power of Learning, Wit, and Skill.

But since *you* carelessly refuse,
    And to my pen the task assign;
O! let your Genius guide my Muse,
    And every vulgar thought refine.

Teach me your best, your best lov'd art,
    With frugal care to store my mind;
In *this* to play the Miser's part,
    And give mean lucre to the wind:

To shun the Coxcomb's empty noise,
    To scorn the Villain's artful mask;
Nor trust gay Pleasure's fleeting joys
    Nor urge Ambition's endless task.

Teach

Teach me to ftem Youth's boifterous tide,
  To regulate its giddy rage;
By Reafon's aid my barque to guide,
  Into the friendly port of Age:

To fhare what *Claffic* Culture yields,
  Thro' *Rhetoric's* painted meads to roam;
With you to reap hiftoric fields,
  And bring the golden Harveft *home.*

To tafte the genuine fweets of *Wit*;
  To quaff in *Humour's* fprightly bowl;
The philofophic *mean* to hit,
  And prize the Dignity of Soul.

Teach me to read fair *Nature's* book,
  Wide opening in each flow'ry plain;
And with judicious eye to look
  On all the glories of her reign.

To hail her, feated on her throne,
  By aweful woods encompafs'd round,
Or her *divine* extraction own,
  Tho' with a wreath of rufhes crown'd.

                              Thro'

Thro' arched walks, o'er spreading lawns,
    Near solemn rocks, with *her* to rove;
Or court her, 'mid her gentle fawns,
    In mossy cell, or maple grove.

Whether the prospect strain the sight,
    Or in the nearer landskips charm,
Where hills, vales, fountains, woods unite,
    To grace your sweet ARCADIAN farm:

There let me sit, and gaze with you,
    On Nature's works by Art refin'd;
And own, while we their contest view,
    Both fair, but fairest, thus combin'd!

An ELEGY on MAN.

WRITTEN JANUARY 1752.

BEHOLD Earth's Lord, imperial Man,
 In ripen'd vigour gay;
His outward form attentive scan,
 And all within survey.

Behold his plans of future life,
 His care, his hope, his love,
Relations dear of child, and wife,
 The dome, the lawn, the grove.

Now see within his active mind,
 More gen'rous passions share,
Friend, neighbour, country, all his kind,
 By turns engage his care.

Behold him range with curious eye,
 O'er Earth from pole to pole,
And thro' th' illimitable sky
 Explore with daring soul.

2   Yet

Yet paſs ſome twenty fleeting years,
 And all his glory flies,
His languid eye is bath'd in tears,
 He ſickens, groans, and dies.

And is this all his deſtin'd lot,
 This all his boaſted ſway?
For ever now to be forgot,
 Amid the mould'ring clay!

Ah gloomy thought! ah worſe than death!
 Life ſickens at the ſound;
Better it were not draw our breath,
 Than run this empty round.

Hence, cheating Fancy, then, awa y
 O let us better try,
By Reaſon's more enlighten'd ray,
 What 'tis indeed to die.

Obſerve yon maſs of putrid earth,
 It holds an embryo-brood,
Ev'n now the reptiles crawl to birth,
 And ſeek their leafy food.

Yet

Yet ftay 'till fome few funs are paft,
  Each forms a filken tomb,
And feems, like man, imprifon'd faft,
  To meet his final doom.

Yet from this filent manfion too
  Anon you fee him rife,
No more a crawling worm to view,
  But tenant of the fkies.

And what forbids that man fhould fhare,
  Some more aufpicious day,
To range at large in open air,
  As light and free as they?

There was a time when life firft warm'd
  Our flefh in fhades of night,
Then was th' imperfect fubftance form'd,
  And fent to view this light.

There was a time, when ev'ry fenfe
  In ftraiter limits dwelt,
Yet each its tafk cou'd then difpenfe,
  We faw, we heard, we felt.

                              And

And times there are, when thro' the veins
   The blood forgets to flow,
Yet then a living pow'r remains,
   Tho' not in active show.

Times too there be, when friendly Sleep's
   Soft charms the Senses bind,
Yet Fancy then her vigils keeps,
   And ranges unconfin'd.

And Reason holds her sep'rate sway,
   Tho' all the Senses wake,
And forms in Mem'ry's storehouse play,
   Of no material make.

What are these then, this eye, this ear,
   But nicer organs found,
A glass to read, a trump to hear,
   The modes of shape, or sound?

And blows may maim, or time impair
   These instruments of clay,
And Death may ravish what they spare,
   Compleating their decay.

                                   But

But are thefe then that living Pow'r
    That thinks, compares, and rules ?
Then fay a fcaffold is a tow'r,
    A workman is his tools.

For aught appears that Death can do,
    That ftill furvives his ftroke,
Its workings plac'd beyond our view,
    Its prefent commerce broke.

But what connections it may find,
    * Boots much to hope, and fear,
And if Inftruction courts the mind,
    'Tis madnefs not to hear.

    * Vid. BUTLER's Analogy.

O

On 'receiving a little IVORY BOX

from a lady,

curiously wrought by her own hands.

LITTLE Box of matchlefs grace!
    Fairer than the faireft face,
Smooth as was her parent-hand,
That did thy wond'rous form command.
Spotlefs as her infant mind,
As her riper age refin'd,
Beauty with the Graces join'd.

    Let me clothe the lovely ftranger,
Let me lodge thee fafe from danger.
Let me guard thy foft repofe,
From giddy Fortune's random blows.
From thoughtlefs mirth, barbaric hate,
From the iron-hand of Fate,
And Oppreffion's deadly weight.

    Thou art not of a fort, or number
Fafhion'd for a Poet's lumber;

Tho'

Tho' more capacious than his purfe,

Too fmall to hold his ftore of verfe.

Too delicate for homely toil,

Too neat for vulgar hands to foil.

  O ! wou'd the Fates permit the Mufe,

Thy future deftiny to chufe !

In thy circle's fairy round,

With a golden fillet bound :

Like the fnow-drop filver white,

Like the glow-worm's humid light,

Like the dew at early dawn,

Like the moon-light on the lawn,

Lucid rows of pearls fhou'd dwell,

Pleas'd as in their native fhell ;

Or the brilliant's fparkling rays,

Shou'd emit a ftarry blaze.

  And if the Fair whofe magic fkill,

Wrought thee paffive to her will,

Deign to regard thy Poet's love,

Nor his afpiring fuit reprove,

Her form fhould crown the fair defign,

Goddefs fit for fuch a fhrine !

     VALEN-

VALENTINE's DAY.

THE tuneful choir in amorous ftrains,
    Accoft their feather'd loves ;
While each fond mate with equal pains,
    The tender fuit approves.

With chearful hop from fpray to fpray,
    They fport along the meads ;
In focial blifs together ftray,
    Where love or fancy leads.

Thro' Spring's gay fcenes each happy pair
    Their fluttering joys purfue ;
Its various charms and produce fhare,
    For ever kind and true.

Their fprightly notes from every fhade,
    Their mutual loves proclaim ;
Till Winter's chilling blafts invade,
    And damp th' enlivening flame.

Then

Then all the jocund fcene declines,
  Nor woods nor meads delight;
The drooping tribe in fecret pines,
  And mourns th' unwelcome fight.

Go, blifsful warblers! timely wife,
  Th' inftructive moral tell!
Nor thou their meaning 'lays defpife,
  My charming ANNABELLE!

HAMLET.'s SOLILOQUY,

IMITATED.

TO *print*, or not to *print*—that is the queftion.
    Whether 'tis better in a trunk to bury
The quirks and crotchets of outrageous fancy,
Or fend a well-wrote copy to the prefs,
And by difclofing, end them? To print, to doubt
No more; and by one act to fay we end
The head-ach, and a thoufand natural fhocks

Of

Of scribbling frenzy—'tis a consummation
Devoutly to be wish'd. To print—to beam
From the same shelf with POPE, in calf well bound:
To sleep, perchance, with QUARLES—Ay, there's the
    rub—
For to what class a writer may be doom'd,
When he hath shuffled off some paltry stuff,
Must give us pause.—There's the respect that makes
Th' unwilling poet keep his piece nine years.
For who wou'd bear th' impatient thirst of fame,
The pride of conscious merit, and 'bove all,
The tedious importunity of friends,
When as himself might his *quietus* make
With a bare inkhorn? Who would fardles bear?
To groan and sweat under a load of wit?
But that the tread of steep PARNASSUS' hill,
That undiscover'd country, with whose bays
Few travellers return, puzzles the will,
And makes us rather bear to live unknown,
Than run the hazard to be known, and damn'd.
Thus Critics do make cowards of us all.
And thus the healthful face of many a poem,

Is

Is fickly'd o'er with a pale manufcript;
And enterprizers of great fire, and fpirit,
With this regard from DODSLEY turn away,
And lofe the name of authors.

R O U N D E L A Y,

WRITTEN FOR THE JUBILEE AT STRAT-
FORD UPON AVON,

CELEBRATED BY MR. GARRICK IN HONOUR
OF SHAKESPEARE, SEPTEMBER 1769.

Set to Mufic by Mr. DIBDIN.

I.

SISTERS of the tuneful train,
  Attend your Parent's jocund ftrain,
'Tis Fancy calls you; follow me
To celebrate the Jubilee.

II. On

II.

On Avon's banks, where SHAKESPEARE's buſt
Points out, and guards his ſleeping duſt;
The ſons of ſcenic mirth agree,
To celebrate the Jubilee.

III.

Come, daughters, come, and bring with you
Th' aerial Sprites and Fairy crew,
And the ſiſter Graces three,
To celebrate the Jubilee.

IV.

Hang around the ſculptur'd tomb
The 'broider'd veſt, the nodding plume,
And the maſk of comic glee,
To celebrate the Jubilee.

V.

From BIRNAM Wood, and BOSWORTH Field,
Bring the ſtandard, bring the ſhield,

With

With drums, and martial fymphony,
To celebrate the Jubilee.

VI.

In mournful numbers now relate
Poor DESDEMONA's haplefs fate,
With frantic deeds of jealoufy,
To celebrate the Jubilee.

VII.

Nor be WINDSOR's Wives forgot,
With their harmlefs merry plot,
The whitening mead, and haunted tree,
To celebrate the Jubilee.

VIII.

Now in jocund ftrains recite
The humours of the braggard Knight,
Fat Knight, and Ancient Piftol he,
To celebrate the Jubilee.

IX. But

IX.

But see in crowds the Gay, the Fair,
To the splendid scene repair,
A scene as fine, as fine can be,
To celebrate the Jubilee.

THE BLACKBIRDS.

AN ELEGY.

THE Sun had chas'd the mountain-snow,
   His beams had pierc'd the stubborn soil,
The melting streams began to flow,
   And Plowmen urg'd their annual toil.

'Twas then, amidst the vocal throng,
   Whom Nature wak'd to mirth, and love,
A Blackbird rais'd his am'rous song,
   And thus it echo'd thro' the grove:

                    O fairest

O faireſt of the feather'd train!
  For whom I ſing, for whom I burn,
Attend with pity to my ſtrain,
  And grant my love a kind return.

For ſee, the wint'ry ſtorms are flown,
  And zephyrs gently fan the air;
Let us the genial influence own,
  Let us the vernal paſtime ſhare.

The Raven plumes his jetty wing,
  To pleaſe his croaking paramour,
The Larks reſponſive carols ſing,
  And tell their paſſion as they ſoar:

But does the Raven's ſable wing
  Excel the gloſſy jet of mine?
Or can the Lark more ſweetly ſing,
  Than we, who ſtrength with ſoftneſs join?

O let me then thy ſteps attend!
  I'll point new treaſures to thy ſight:
Whether the grove thy wiſh befriend,
  Or hedge-rows green, or meadows bright.

I'll

I'll guide thee to the cleareſt rill,

    Whoſe ſtreams among the pebbles ſtray;

There will we ſip, and ſip our fill,

    Or on the flow'ry margin play.

I'll lead thee to the thickeſt brake,

    Impervious to the ſchool-boy's eye;

For thee the plaiſter'd neſt I'll make,

    And to thy downy boſom fly.

When, prompted by a mother's care,

    Thy warmth ſhall form th' impriſon'd young,

The pleaſing taſk I'll gladly ſhare,

    Or cheer thy labours with a ſong.

To bring thee food I'll range the fields,

    And cull the beſt of ev'ry kind,

Whatever Nature's bounty yields,

    And love's aſſiduous care can find.

And when my lovely mate wou'd ſtray,

    To taſte the ſummer ſweets at large,

I'll wait at home the live-long day,

    And fondly tend our little charge.

Then

Then prove with me the sweets of love,
    With me divide the cares of life,
No bush shall boast in all the grove,
    A mate so fond, so blest a wife.

He ceas'd his song—the plumy dame
    Heard with delight the love-sick strain,
Nor long conceal'd a mutual flame,
    Nor long repress'd his am'rous pain.

He led her to the nuptial bow'r,
    And perch'd with triumph by her side ;
What gilded roof cou'd boast that hour
    A fonder mate, or happier bride?

Next morn he wak'd her with a song,
    Behold, he said, the new-born day,
The Lark his mattin-peal has rung,
    Arise, my love, and come away.

Together thro' the fields they stray'd,
    And to the murm'ring riv'let's side,
Renew'd their vows, and hopp'd, and play'd
    With artless joy, and decent pride.

                    When

When O! with grief my Muse relates
　　What dire misfortune clos'd the tale,
Sent by an order from the Fates,
　　A Gunner met them in the vale.

Alarm'd, the lover cried, My dear,
　　Haste, haste away, from danger fly;
Here, Gunner, point thy thunder here,
　　O spare my love, and let me die.

'At him the Gunner took his aim,
　　Too sure the volley'd thunder flew!
O had he chose some other game,
　　Or shot—as he was wont to do!

Divided Pair! forgive the wrong,
　　While I with tears your fate rehearse,
I'll join the Widow's plaintive song,
　　And save the Lover in my verse.

THE

The GOLDFINCHES.

An ELEGY.

TO WILLIAM SHENSTONE, ESQ.

Ingenuas didiciffe fideliter artes
Emollit mores, nec finit effe feros.

TO you, whofe groves protect the feather'd choirs,
  Who lend their artlefs notes a willing ear,
To you, whom Pity moves, and Tafte infpires,
  The Doric ftrain belongs, O SHENSTONE hear.

'Twas gentle Spring, when all the plumy race,
  By Nature taught in nuptial leagues combine,
A Goldfinch joy'd to meet the warm embrace,
  And with her mate in Love's delights to join.

All in a garden, on a currant-bufh,
  With wond'rous art they built their airy feat;
In the next orchard liv'd a friendly Thrufh,
  Nor diftant far a Woodlark's foft retreat.

i

Here

Here bleſt with eaſe, and in each other bleſt,

    With early ſongs they wak'd the neighb'ring groves,

Till time matur'd their joys, and crown'd their neſt .

    With infant pledges of their faithful loves.

And now what tranſport glow'd in either's eye?

    What equal fondneſs dealt th' allotted food?

What joy each other's likeneſs to deſcry,

    And future ſonnets in the chirping brood!

But ah! what earthly happineſs can laſt?

    How does the faireſt purpoſe often fail?

A truant ſchoolboy's wantonneſs cou'd blaſt

    Their flatt'ring hopes, and leave them both to wail.

The moſt ungentle of his tribe was he,

    No gen'rous precept ever touch'd his heart,

With concord falſe, and hideous proſody

    He ſcrawl'd his taſk, and blunder'd o'er his part.

On miſchief bent, he mark'd, with rav'nous eyes,

    Where wrapt in down the callow ſongſters lay,

Then ruſhing, rudely ſeiz'd the glitt'ring prize,

    And bore it in his impious hands away!

                               But

But how fhall I defcribe, in numbers rude,
  The pangs for poor CHRYSOMITRIS decreed;
When from her fecret ftand aghaft fhe view'd
  The cruel fpoiler perpetrate the deed?

O grief of griefs! with fhrieking voice fhe cried;
  What fight is this that I have liv'd to fee!
O! that I had in Youth's fair feafon died,
  From Love's falfe joys, and bitter forrows free.

Was it for this, alas! with weary bill,
  Was it for this I pois'd th' unwieldy ftraw?
For this I bore the mofs from yonder hill,
  Nor fhun'd the pond'rous ftick along to draw?

Was it for this I pick'd the wool with care,
  Intent with nicer fkill our work to crown?
For this, with pain, I bent the ftubborn hair,
  And lin'd our cradle with the thiftle's down? -

Was it for this my freedom I refign'd,
  And ceas'd to rove at large from plain to plain?
For this I fate at home whole days confin'd,
  To bear the fcorching heat, and pealing rain?

P   Was

Was it for this my watchful eyes grow dim?

 For this the rofes on my cheek turn pale?

Pale is my golden plumage, once fo trim!

 And all my wonted mirth, and fpirits fail!

O Plund'rer vile! O more than Adders fell!

 More murth'rous than the Cat, with prudifh face!

Fiercer than Kites in whom the Furies dwell,

 And thievifh as the Cuckow's pilf'ring race!

May juicy plumbs for thee forbear to grow,

 For thee no flow'r unveil its charming dies;

May birch-trees thrive to work thee fharper woe,

 And lift'ning ftarlings mock thy frantic cries.

Thus fang the mournful bird her piteous tale,

 The piteous tale her mournful mate return'd,

Then fide by fide they fought the diftant vale,

 And there in fecret fadnefs inly mourn'd.

THE

The SWALLOWS:

An ELEGY.

PART I.

ERE yellow Autumn from our plains retir'd,
    And gave to wintry ſtorms the varied year,
The Swallow-race with preſcient gift inſpir'd,
    To ſouthern climes prepar'd their courſe to ſteer.

On DAMON's roof a large aſſembly ſate,
    His roof a refuge to the feather'd kind!
With ſerious look he mark'd the grave debate,
    And to his DELIA thus addreſs'd his mind.

Obſerve yon' twitt'ring flock, my gentle maid!
    Obſerve, and read the wond'rous ways of Heav'n!
With us thro' Summer's genial reign they ſtay'd,
    And food, and ſunſhine to their wants were giv'n.

But

But now, by fecret inftinct taught, they know
   The near approach of elemental ftrife,
Of bluft'ring tempefts, and of chilling fnow,
   With ev'ry pang, and fcourge of tender life.

Thus warn'd they meditate a fpeedy flight,
   For this ev'n now they prune their vig'rous wing,
For this each other to the toil excite,
   And prove their ftrength in many a fportive ring.

No forrow loads their breaft, or dims their eye,
   To quit their wonted haunts, or native home,
Nor fear they launching on the boundlefs fky,
   In fearch of future fettlements to roam.

They feel a pow'r, an impulfe all divine,
   That warns them hence, they feel it, and obey,
To this direction all their cares refign,
   Unknown their deftin'd ftage, unmark'd their way.

Peace to your flight! ye mild, domeftic race!
   O! for your wings to travel with the fun!
Health brace your nerves, and zephyrs aid your pace,
   Till your long voyage happily be done.

                           See

See, DELIA, on my roof your guefts to-day,
  To-morrow on my roof your guefts no more,
Ere yet 'tis night with hafte they wing away,
  To-morrow lands them on fome happier fhore.

How juft the moral in this fcene convey'd!
  And what without a moral? wou'd we read!
Then mark what DAMON tells his gentle maid,
  And with his leffon regifter the deed.

So youthful joys fly like the Summer's gale,
  So threats the winter of inclement age,
Life's bufy plot a fhort, fantaftic tale!
  And Nature's changeful fcenes the fhifting ftage!

* And does no friendly pow'r to man difpenfe
  The joyful tidings of fome happier clime?
Find we no guide in gracious Providence
  Beyond the gloomy grave, and fhort-liv'd time?

---

* This little piece, and its companions, particularly the
following, are highly honour'd by Mr. AIKIN, in his ingenious and entertaining "Effay on the Application of
Natural Hiftory to Poetry."

Yes,

Yes, yes the facred oracles we hear,

    That point the path to realms of endlefs joy,

That bid our trembling hearts no danger fear,

    Tho' clouds furround, and angry fkies annoy.

Then let us wifely for our flight prepare,

    Nor count this ftormy world our fixt abode,

Obey the call, and truft our Leader's care,

    To fmooth the rough, and light the darkfome road.

Moses, by grant divine, led Israel's hoft

    Thro' dreary paths to Jordan's fruitful fide;

But we a loftier theme than theirs can boaft,

    A better promife, and a nobler guide.

The SWALLOWS.

PART II.

AT length the Winter's howling blafts are o'er,

    Array'd in fmiles the lovely Spring returns,

Now fewel'd hearths attractive blaze no more,

    And ev'ry breaft with inward fervor burns.

                    Again

Again the daisies peep, the violets blow,
 Again the vocal tenants of the grove
Forgot the patt'ring hail, or driving snow,
 Renew the lay to melody, and love.

And see, my DELIA, see o'er yonder stream,
 Where, on the bank, the lambs in gambols play,
Alike attracted by the sunny gleam,
 Again the Swallows take their wonted way.

Welcome, ye gentle tribe, your sports pursue,
 Welcome again to DELIA, and to me,
Your peaceful councils on my roof renew,
 And plan new settlements from danger free.

Again I'll listen to your grave debates,
 Again I'll hear your twitt'ring songs unfold
What policy directs your wand'ring states,
 What bounds are settled, and what tribes enroll'd.

Again I'll hear you tell of distant lands,
 What insect-nations rise from EGYPT's mud,
What painted swarms subsist on LYBIA's sands,
 What GANGES yields, and what th' EUPHRATEAN
  flood.

P 4   Thrice

Thrice happy race ! whom Nature's call invites
 To travel o'er her realms with active wing,
To taste her various stores, her best delights,
 The Summer's radiance, and the sweets of Spring:

While we are doom'd to bear the restless change
 Of varying seasons, vapours dank, and dry,
Forbid like you in milder climes to range,
 When wintry storms usurp the low'ring sky.

Yet know the period to your joys assign'd,
 Know ruin hovers o'er this earthly ball,
As lofty tow'rs stoop prostrate to the wind,
 Its secret props of adamant shall fall.

But when yon' radiant sun shall shine no more,
 The spirit, freed from sin's tyrannic sway,
On lighter pinions borne than yours, shall soar
 To fairer realms beneath a brighter ray.

To plains ethereal, and celestial bow'rs,
 Where wintry storms no rude access obtain,
Where blasts no lightning, and no tempest low'rs,
 But ever-smiling Spring, and Pleasure reign.

THE END.

A D A M:

OR, THE

Fatal Difobedience,

An O R A T O R I O,

COMPILED FROM THE

PARADISE LOST

OF

M I L T O N.

AND ADAPTED TO MUSIC.

By R. J.

MAN;

OF THE

Fatal Disobedience;

ORATORIO.

compiled from the

PARADISE LOST

OF

MILTON

ADAPTED TO MUSIC

BY R. J.

ADVERTISEMENT.

THE *Comus, Allegro, Il Penserofo, Lyci-das,* and *Samfon-Agoniftes* of MILTON, have each of them had the good fortune to be made choice of as proper fubjects for mufical compofition ; but no one appears hitherto to have entertained any thoughts of adapting any part of *Paradife Loft* to the fame ufe, though confeffedly the moft capital of all his works, and containing the greateft variety both of fentiment, and language fuf-ceptible of the graces of that harmonious art *. Indeed the plan for this purpofe was

not

---

* What Dr. GREGORY fays of Religion in general as a fubject for mufical compofition, may be applied with the ftricteft propriety to this work in particular, viz. that it affords

not fo obvious. The others were in a great meafure ready prepared to the compofer's hands; here the cafe was different. The feveral beautiful paffages contained in this poem lay fcattered through a wide compafs, and it appear'd difficult to affemble, and unite them into any regular, and compendious form adapted to public reprefentation. This the compiler has attempted, by confining himfelf to thofe paffages which have a more immediate reference to the principal ftory, and omitting what was more remote, and digreffive. In executing this defign he has varied as little as was poffible from the order of time, and language of MILTON, and endeavour'd not to offend the judgment, at

affords almoft all the variety of fubjects which mufic can exprefs; the fublime, the joyous, the cheerful, the ferene, the devout, the plaintive, the melancholy.

Comparative View of the State and Faculties of Man, page 73, 74.

the

the fame time that he confulted the entertainment of the public.

He will not fay that he has omitted no particular beauties of this poem, for not to do this would be to tranfcribe the whole; but he can truly fay that he has taken fome pains to include as many as could with any propriety be brought within the compafs of his undertaking, and that it will be no fmall pleafure to him to be the occafion of making them more univerfally admired, by means of an alliance with that fifter-art, whofe expreffive ftrains are the only additional ornament of which they were capable.

So far was written after the following piece was entirely finifh'd, and at a time when the compiler thought that no one had engaged

gaged in the fame defign. In this however he finds he was miftaken, and can truly fay, that had he been fo much converfant in the mufical world as to have known more early that a perfon of Mr. STILLINGFLEET's me+ rit, and abilities had undertaken this work, he would certainly have declined it : but having fpent fome time in it, and finding that this gentleman's plan does not entirely coincide with his, he hopes he may be ex- cufed for prefenting it to the world after him.

He will no further detain the reader than to fay, that his aim was to furnifh the com- pofer with MILTON's own beauties, fo adapted as that the capital lines and moft ftriking fentiments might naturally offer themfelves to mufical diftinction, rather than form words for that purpofe, as he thought

had

had been done in other compofitions of a like nature, in a manner very forced, and unnatural; and where, though the ear is gratified, the underftanding is generally dif-gufted.

The

The Perſons here repreſented are

ADAM, and
EVE; with the
GUARDIAN ANGELS of Paradiſe, and others.

The Scene is PARADISE.

A D A M:

AN

O R A T O R I O.

ACT I.

SCENE I.

RECITATIVE.

UNDER a tuft of shade, that, on a green,
    Stood whisp'ring soft, on EDEN's blissful plain,
Sate the first human Pair. (Not that fair Field
Of ENNA, where PROSERPINE, gath'ring flow'rs,
Herself, a fairer flow'r, by gloomy DIS
Was gather'd; nor that sweet ELYSIAN Grove
Of DAPHNE by ORONTES, and th' inspir'd

Q   CASTALIAN

CASTALIAN Spring, might with this Paradife
Of EDEN ftrive: nor that NYSEAN Ifle,
Girt with the river TRITON, where old CHAM,
Whom Gentiles AMMON call, and LYBIAN JOVE,
Hid AMALTHEA, and her florid fon,
Young BACCHUS from his ftep-dame RHEA's eye—
Nor where ABASSINE kings their iffue guard,
Mount AMARA! enclos'd with fhining rock,
A whole day's journey high.)   Around them grew
All trees of nobleft kind for fight, fmell, tafte,
And all amid them grew the Tree of Life,
High eminent, blooming ambrofial fruit
Of vegetable gold; and, next to Life,
Our Death! the Tree of Knowledge grew faft by.
Here waving boughs wept od'rous gums, and balm:
On others fruit, burnifh'd with golden rind,
Hung amiable: betwixt them lawns, and downs,
Or palmy hillock, or the flow'ry lap
Of fome irriguous valley fpread her ftore,
Flow'rs of all hues, and without thorn the rofe.
Another fide umbrageous grots, and caves
Of cool recefs! o'er which the mantling vine

Lays

Lays forth her purple grape, and gently creeps
Luxuriant. Mean while murm'ring waters fall
Down the flope hills difpers'd, or, in a lake,
That to the fringed bank, with myrtle crown'd,
Her cryftal mirrour holds, unite their ftreams.
The birds their quire apply—airs, vernal airs
Breathing the fmell of field, or grove attune
The trembling leaves, and whifper whence they ftole
Their balmy fpoils. About them frifking play'd
All beafts of th' earth, fince wild, and of all chafe
In wood, or wildernefs, foreft, or den.
Sporting the lion ramp'd, and, in his paw,
Dandled the kid. Bears, tygers, ounces, pards
Gambol'd before them. Th' unwieldy elephant,
To make them mirth, us'd all his might, and wreath'd
His lithe probofcis. Clofe the ferpent fly,
Infinuating, wove, with Gordian twine,
His braided train, and, of his fatal guile
Gave proof unheeded. They fuperior fate
As lords of all, of God-like fhape erect!
For valour he, and contemplation form'd,
For foftnefs fhe, and fweet attractive grace!

AIR.

A I R.

" They fuperior fate,
" As lords of all, of God-like fhape erect !
" For valour he, and comtemplation form'd,
" For foftnefs fhe, and fweet attractive grace !"

S C E N E   II.

RECITATIVE.

On the foft downy bank, damafkt with flow'rs,
Reclin'd they fate, when ADAM firft of men
To firft of women EVE thus fmiling fpake.

A D A M.

Sole partner, and fole part of all thefe joys,
Dearer thyfelf than all! needs muft the Pow'r,
That made us, and, for us, this ample world,
Be infinitely good, and, of his good
As liberal, and free as infinite;
Who rais'd us from the duft, and plac'd us here,

In

In all this happiness; who yet requires
From us no other service, than to keep
This one, this easy charge—Of all the Trees
In PARADISE, that bear delicious fruit
So various, not to taste that only Tree
Of Knowledge, planted by the Tree of Life.

SONG.

" Then let us ever praise Him, and extol
" His bounty, following our delightful task,
" To prune these growing plants, and tend these
      " flow'rs,
" Which, were it toilsome, yet with thee were sweet."

RECITATIVE.

E V E.

              O thou! for whom
And from whom I was form'd! Flesh of thy flesh!
And without whom am to no end! My guide,
And head! what thou hast said is just, and right:
For we indeed to Him all praises owe,

And

And daily thanks: I chiefly, who enjoy
So much the happier lot, enjoying thee.

AFFETUOSO.

" That day I oft remember, when from ſleep
" I firſt awak'd, and found myſelf repos'd
" Under a ſhade of flow'rs, much wond'ring where,
" And what I was, whence thither brought, and how.
" Not diſtant far from thence, a murm'ring ſound
" Of waters iſſued from a cave, and ſpread
" Into a liquid plain, then ſtood unmov'd
" Pure as th' expanſe of Heav'n. I thither went,
" With unexperienc'd thought, and laid me down
" On the green bank to look into the clear,
" Smooth lake, that to me ſeem'd another ſky.
" As I bent down to look, juſt oppoſite,
" A ſhape within the watry gleam appear'd,
" Bending to look on me. I ſtarted back,
" It ſtarted back. But pleas'd I ſoon return'd,
" Pleas'd it return'd as ſoon, with anſw'ring looks
" Of ſympathy, and love. There I had fix'd
" Mine eyes till now, and pin'd with vain deſire,

" Had

" Had not a voice thus warn'd me. What thou fee'ft,

" What there thou fee'ft, fair creature! is thyfelf.

" With thee it came, and goes. But follow me,

" And I will bring thee where no fhadow ftays

" Thy coming, and thy foft embraces—He!

" Whofe image thou art—him thou fhalt enjoy

" Infeparably thine, to him fhalt bear

" Multitudes like thyfelf, and thence be call'd

" Mother of human race. What cou'd I do,

" But follow ftrait, invifibly thus led?

" Till I efpied thee, fair, indeed, and tall,

" Under a platan. Yet methought lefs fair,

" Lefs winning foft, lefs amiably mild,

" Than that fmooth watry image. Back I turn'd.

" Thou following cry'dft aloud;

AIR.

" Return, fair Eve!

" Whom fly'ft thou? whom thou fly'ft, of him thou

" art,

" His flefh, his bone! To give thee being I lent

" Out of my fide to thee, neareft my heart,

Q 4 " Subftantial

" Subſtantial life, to have thee by my ſide,

" Henceforth an individual ſolace dear.

" Part of my ſoul I ſeek thee, and thee claim

" My other half." With that thy gentle hand

" Seiz'd mine ; I yielded—and from that time ſee

" How beauty is excell'd by manly grace,

" And wiſdom, which alone is truly fair."

RECITATIVE.

So ſpake our gen'ral Mother, and with eyes

Of conjugal affection, unreprov'd,

And meek ſurrender, half embracing lean'd

On our firſt Father. Half her ſwelling breaſt

Naked met his, under the flowing gold

Of her looſe treſſes hid. He, in delight

Both of her beauty, and ſubmiſſive charms,

Smil'd with ſuperior love, and preſs'd her lip

With kiſſes pure. Thus they in am'rous ſport,

As well beſeems fair couple, linkt as they,

In happy nuptial league, their minutes paſs'd,

Crown'd with ſublime delight. The lovelieſt pair

That ever yet in Love's embraces met :

ADAM

ADAM the goodlieft man of men fince born
His fons, the faireft of her daughters EVE !

CHORUS.

" Hail! HYMEN's firft, accomplifh'd Pair !
  " Goodlieft he of all his fons !
  " Of her daughters fhe moft fair !
    " Goodlieft he !
    " She moft fair !
  " Goodlieft he of all his fons !
  " Of her daughters fhe moft fair.

SCENE III.

RECITATIVE.

Now came ftill Ev'ning on, and Twilight grey
Had, in her fober liv'ry all things clad.
Silence accompanied : for beaft, and bird,
They to their graffy couch, thefe to their nefts
Were flunk : all but the wakeful Nightingale !
She all night long her am'rous defcant fung.

Silence

Silence was pleas'd. Now glow'd the firmament

With living faphires. Hefperus, that led

The ftarry hoft, rode brighteft, till the Moon,

Rifing in clouded majefty, at length,

Apparent queen! unveil'd her peerlefs light,

And o'er the dark her filver mantle threw.

When ADAM thus to EVE.

A D A M.

　　　　　　　　　　　Fair Confort! th' hour

Of Night, and all things now retir'd to reft

Mind us of like repofe: fince God hath fet

Labour, and reft as day, and night to men

Succeffive, and the timely due of fleep,

Now falling with foft flumb'rous weight, inclines

Our eye-lids. Ere frefh Morning ftreak the eaft

With firft approach of light, we muft be ris'n,

And at our pleafant labour, to reform

Yon' flow'ry arbours, yonder alleys green,

Our walk at Noon, with branches overgrown.

Mean while, as Nature wills, Night bids us reft.

E V E.

E V E.

My author, and difpofer, what thou bid'ft
Unargu'd I obey, fo God ordains.
God is thy law, thou mine. To know no more
Is woman's happieft knowledge, and her praife.

A I R.

" With thee converfing, I forget all time.
" All feafons, and their change, all pleafe alike.
" Sweet is the breath of Morn, her rifing fweet,
" With charm of earlieft birds ! Pleafant the Sun !
" When firft on this delightful land he fpreads
" His orient beams on herb, tree, fruit, and flow'r,
" Glift'ring with dew : fragrant the fertile Earth,
" After foft fhow'rs ! and fweet the coming on
" Of grateful Evening mild ; the filent Night,
" With this her folemn bird ; and this fair Moon,
" And thofe the gems of Heav'n, her ftarry train !
" But neither breath of Morn, when fhe afcends,
" With charm of earlieft birds, nor rifing Sun
" On this delightful land, nor herb, fruit, flow'r,

" Glift'ring

" Glift'ring with dew, nor fragrance after fhow'rs,

" Nor grateful Evening mild, nor filent Night,

" With this her folemn bird, nor walk by Moon,

" Or glitt'ring ftar-light without thee is fweet."

RECITATIVE.

Thus talking, hand in hand, alone they pafs'd

On to their blifsful bow'r.   It was a place,

Chos'n by the Sov'reign Planter, when he fram'd

All things to man's delightful ufe; the roof,

Of thickeft covert, was in-woven fhade,

Laurel, and myrtle, and what higher grew.

Of firm, and fragrant leaf; on either fide,

Acanthus, and each od'rous, bufhy fhrub

Fenc'd up the verdant wall, each beauteous flow'r,

Iris, all hues, rofes, and jeffamine

Rear'd high their flourifh'd heads between, and wrought

Mofaic; under foot the violet,

Crocus, and hyacinth, with rich inlay,

Broider'd the ground, more colour'd than with ftone

Of

Of coftlieft emblem. · Other creature here
Beaft, bird, infect, or worm, durft enter none,
Such was their awe of Man. In fhady bow'r,
More facred, and fequefter'd; tho' but feign'd,
PAN, or SYLVANUS never flept, nor Nymph,
Or Faunus haunted. Here, in clofe recefs,
With flow'rs, and garlands, and fweet fmelling
    herbs
Efpoufed EVE deck'd firft her nuptial bed,
And heav'nly quires the Hymenæan fung.

    Thus at their fhady lodge arriv'd, both ftood,
Both turn'd, and, under open Sky, ador'd
The God that made both Sky, Air, Earth, and Heav'n,
Which they beheld, the Moon's refplendent globe,
And ftarry pole.

EVENING HYMN.

    " Thou alfo mad'ft the night,
" Maker omnipotent! and Thou the day,
" Which we, in our appointed work employ'd,
" Have finifh'd, happy in our mutual help,

                  And

" And mutual love, the crown of all our blifs;

" Ordain'd by Thee, and this delicious place,

" For us too large, where Thy abundance wants

" Partakers, and uncropt falls to the ground.

" But Thou haft promis'd from us two a race,

" To fill the earth, who fhall, with us, extol

" Thy goodnefs infinite, both when we wake,

" And when we feek, as now, thy gift of Sleep.

END OF THE FIRST ACT.

A C T II.

S C E N E I.

RECITATIVE.

O ! For that warning voice, which he, who faw
Th' Apocalyps, heard cry in Heav'n aloud,
Then when the Dragon, put to fecond rout,
Came furious down, to be reveng'd on men,
Woe to th' inhabitants of th' earth ! that now,
While time was, our firft Parents had been warn'd
The coming of their fecret foe, and fcap'd,
Haply fo fcap'd his mortal fnare; for now
Satan, now firft inflam'd with rage, came down,
The tempter, ere th' accufer of mankind.

CHORUS.

He, who fits enthron'd on high,
Above the circle of the fky,

3   Sees

Sees his rage, and mocks his toil,
Which on himfelf fhall foon recoil:
In the fnare, with malice, wrought
For others, fhall his feet be caught.

S C E N E   II.

R E C I T A T I V E.

Now Morn her rofy fteps in th' eaftern clime
Advancing, fow'd the earth with orient pearl,
When ADAM wak'd, fo cuftom'd, for his fleep
Was airy light, from pure digeftion bred,
And temp'rate vapours bland, which th' only found
Of leaves, and fuming rills, AURORA's fan,
Lightly difpers'd, and the fhrill matin fong
Of birds on ev'ry bough.   Unwaken'd EVE
Clofe at his fide, in naked beauty lay,
Beauty! which, whether waking, or afleep,
Shot forth peculiar charms.   He, on his fide,
Leaning, half rais'd, with looks of cordial love
Hung over her enamour'd: then, with voice,

                                        Mild

Mild as when ZEPHYRUS on FLORA breathes,
Her hand soft-touching, whisper'd thus.

SONG.

"Awake!

" My faireſt, my eſpous'd, my lateſt found,

" Heav'n's laſt, beſt gift, my ever newdelight,

" Awake! the morning ſhines, and the freſh field

" Calls us; we loſe the prime, to mark how ſpring

" Our tended plants, how blows the citron grove,

" What drops the myrrh, and what the balmy reed;

" How Nature paints her colours; how the bee

" Sits on the bloom, extracting liquid ſweets."

RECITATIVE.

E V E.

ADAM! well may we labour ſtill to dreſs
This garden, ſtill to tend, herb, plant, and flow'r,
Our pleaſant taſk enjoin'd! but till more hands
Aid us, the work under our labour grows
Luxurious by reſtraint. Let us divide
Our labours then, for while together thus
Our taſk we chooſe, what wonder if ſo near

R   Looks

Looks intervene, and fmiles, or object new
Cafual difcourfe draw on, which intermits
Our day's work, brought to little, though begun
Early, and th' hour of fupper comes unearn'd.

A D A M.

　　Thefe paths, and bow'rs doubt not but our joint
　　　　hands
Will keep from wildernefs with eafe as wide
As we need walk, till younger hands ere long
Affift us.　But if much converfe perhaps
Thee fatiate, to fhort abfence I cou'd yield,
For folitude fometimes is beft fociety,
And fhort retirement urges fweet return.
But other doubt poffeffes me, left harm
Befal thee fever'd from me; for thou know'ft
What hath been warn'd us, what malicious foe,
Envying our happinefs, and of his own
Defpairing, feeks to work us woe, and fhame,
By fly affault; and fomewhere, nigh at hand,
Watches no doubt, with greedy hope, to find
His wifh, and beft advantage! us afunder;

　　　　　　　　Hopelefs

Hopeless to circumvent us join'd, where each
To other speedy aid might lend at need.
Then leave not, I advise, the faithful side
Which gave thee being, shades thee, and protects.

A I R.

" The wife, where danger, or dishonour lurks,
" Safest, and seemliest near her husband stays,
" Who guards her; or with her the worst endures."

RECITATIVE.

E V E.

Offspring of Heav'n, and Earth, and all Earth's
Lord!
That such an enemy we have, who seeks
Our ruin, oft inform'd by thee, I learn.
But that thou shou'dst my firmness therefore doubt,
To God, or thee, because we have a foe
May tempt it, I expected not to hear.

A D A M.

Daughter of God, and man, immortal EVE!
For such thou art, from sin, and blame entire:

R 2   Not

Not diffident of thee, do I diffuade

Thy abfence from my fight, but to avoid

Th' attempt, which thou thyfelf with virtuous fcorn

And anger wou'd'ft refent. Mifdeem not then,

If fuch affront I labour to avert

From thee alone, which on us both at once

The enemy, tho' bold, will hardly dare,

Or daring, firft on me th' affault fhall light.

Nor thou his malice, and falfe guile contemn.

Subtle he needs muft be, who cou'd feduce

Angels ; nor think fuperfluous others aid.

" I, from the influence of thy looks, receive

" Accefs in ev'ry virtue ; in thy fight,

" More wife, more watchful, ftronger, if need were,

" Of outward ftrength; while fhame, thou look-

    ing on,

" Shame to be overcome, or over-reach'd !

" Wou'd utmoft vigour raife, and rais'd unite."

Why fhou'd'ft not thou like fenfe within thee feel,

When I am prefent, and thy trial chufe

With me, beft witnefs of thy virtue tried?

                                                EVE.

E V E.

If this be our condition, thus to dwell
In narrow circuit, ftraiten'd by a foe,
Subtle, or violent, we not endued,
Single, with like defence, wherever met,
How are we happy, ftill in fear of harm?

A I R.

" Frail is our happinefs, if this be fo,
" And EDEN were no EDEN thus expos'd."

R E C I T A T I V E.

A D A M.

O woman! beft are all things, as the will
Of God ordain'd them. His creating hand
Nothing imperfect, or deficient left
Of all that he created, much lefs Man,
Or aught that might his happy ftate fecure:
Secure from outward force. Within himfelf
The danger lies, yet lies within his pow'r.

R 3   Againft

Againſt his will he can receive no harm;

But God left free the will, for what obeys

Reaſon is free, and reaſon he made right,

And bid her ſtill beware, and ſtill erect,

Leſt by ſome fair, appearing good ſurpriz'd,

She dictate falſe, and miſinform the will

To do what God exprefsly hath forbid.

Not then miſtruſt, but tender love enjoins

That I ſhou'd mind thee oft, and mind thou me,

Firm we ſubſiſt, yet poffible to ſwerve.

A I R.

" But if thou think'ſt trial unfought may find

" Us both ſecurer, than thus warn'd thou ſeem'ſt,

" Go! for thy ſtay, not free, abſents thee more.

" Go in thy native innocence. Rely

" On what thou haſt of virtue: ſummon all,

" For God towards thee hath done his part, do thine."

SCENE

SCENE III.

RECITATIVE.

So hafte they to the field, their pleafing tafk!
But firft, from under fhady, arb'rous roof,
Soon as they forth were come to open fight
Of day-fpring, and the Sun, who fcarce upris'n,
With wheels yet hov'ring o'er the ocean brim,
Shot parallel to th' earth his dewy ray,
Difcov'ring, in wide circuit, all the bounds
Of PARADISE, and EDEN's happy plains,
Lowly they bow'd adoring, and began
Their orifons, each morning duly paid,
In various ftyle: for neither various ftyle
Nor holy rapture wanted they to praife
Their Maker in fit ftrains, pronounc'd, or fung,
Unmeditated; fuch prompt eloquence
Flow'd from their lips, in profe, or num'rous verfe,
More tuneable than needed lute, or harp
To add more fweetnefs: and they thus began.

MORNING

MORNING HYMN.

" Thefe are Thy glorious works, Parent of good,

" Almighty ! Thine this univerfal frame !

" Thus wond'rous fair ! Thyfelf how wond'rous then !

" Unfpeakable ! who fit'ft above thefe heav'ns,

" To us invifible ; or dimly feen

" In thefe Thy loweft works : yet thefe declare

" Thy goodnefs beyond thought, and pow'r divine.

   " Speak ye, who beft can tell, ye fons of light !

" Angels, for ye behold Him, and, with fongs,

" And choral fymphonies day without night,

" Circle His throne rejoicing ; ye in heav'n,

" On earth join all ye creatures to extol

" Him firft, Him laft, Him midft, and without end,

   " Faireft of Stars, laft in the train of night,

" If better thou belong not to the dawn,

" Sure pledge of day ! that crown'ft the fmiling morn

" With thy bright circlet, praife Him in thy fphere,

" While day arifes, that fweet hour of prime.

   " Thou Sun, both eye, and foul of this great world !

" Acknowledge Him thy greater, found His praife

                                                    In

" In thy eternal courfe, both when thou climb'ft,

" And when high noon haft gain'd, and when haft
    " fall'n.

" Moon! that now meet'ft the orient Sun, now
    " fly'ft

" With the fixt ftars, fixt in their orb that flies,

" And ye five other wand'ring fires, that move

" In myftic dance, not without fong, refound

" His praife, who out of darknefs call'd up light;

" Air! and ye Elements, the eldeft birth

" Of Nature's womb, that, in quaternion, run

" Perpetual circle multiform, and mix,

" And nourifh all things, let your ceafelefs change

" Vary to your great Maker ftill new praife.

" Ye Mifts, and Exhalations that now rife,

" From hill, or fteaming lake, dufky, or grey,

" Till the Sun paint your fleecy fkirts with gold,

" In honour to the world's great Maker rife,

" Whether to deck with clouds th' uncolour'd fky,

" Or wet the thirfty earth with falling fhow'rs,

" Rifing, or falling ftill advance His praife.

" His

" His praife, ye Winds, that from four quarters blow,

" Breathe foft, or loud; and wave your tops, ye pines,

" With ev'ry plant, in fign of honour wave.

   " Fountains! and ye that warble, as ye flow,

" Melodious murmurs, warbling tune His praife.

   " Join voices, all ye living fouls! ye birds!

" That finging, up to Heav'n's bright gates afcend,

" Bear on your wings, and in your notes His praife.

   " Ye that in waters glide, and ye that walk

" The earth; and ftately tread, or lowly creep,

" Witnefs if I be filent morn, or ev'n,

" To hill, or valley, fountain, or frefh fhade

" Made vocal by my fong, and taught His praife.

   " Hail, univerfal Lord! be bounteous ftill

" To give us only good; and, if the night

" Have gather'd aught of evil, or conceal'd,

" Difperfe it, as now light difpels the dark."

RECITATIVE.

So pray'd they innocent; then to their tafk
They diff'rent ways repair—he, where his choice

Leads

Leads him, or where moſt needs, whether to wind
The woodbine round his arbour, or direct
The claſping ivy where to twine; while ſhe
In yonder ſpring of roſes, intermixt
With myrtle, ſeeks what to redreſs till noon,
Her long, with ardent look, his eye purſu'd
Delighted, but deſiring more her ſtay.
She, like a wood-nymph light of DELIA's train,
Betook her to the groves, but DELIA's ſelf
In gait ſurpaſs'd, and goddeſs-like deport.
Grace was in all her ſteps, Heav'n in her eye;
In ev'ry geſture dignity, and love.

AIR.

" Grace was in all her ſteps, Heav'n in her eye;
" In ev'ry geſture dignity, and love."

END OF ACT THE SECOND.

ACT

ACT III.

SCENE I.

The GUARDIAN ANGELS.

RECITATIVE.

OUR charge, tho' unfuccefsful, is fulfill'd.

　　The Tempter hath prevail'd, and Man is fall'n.

Earth felt the wound, and Nature, from her feat

Sighing thro' all her works, gave figns of woe,

That all was loft. The fatal omens reach'd

Our glitt'ring files, and thro' th' angelic guard

Spread fadnefs, mixt with pity, not with guilt,

Or confcious negligence. After fhort paufe,

Earth trembled from her entrails, as again

In pangs, and Nature gave a fecond groan ;

Sky lower'd, and, mutt'ring thunder, fome fad drops

Wept at compleating of the mortal fin.

Now up to Heav'n we hafte, before the throne

Supreme, t' approve our faithful vigilance.

CHORUS.

CHORUS.

" Righteous art thou, O Lord ! and juſt are thy
   " judgments.

     "HALLELUJAH!"

RECITATIVE.

But ſee ! with viſage diſcompos'd, and dim'd
With paſſions foul, like this late azure clime
With clouds, and ſtorms o'ercaſt, the human pair
Bend hitherward their ſteps diſconſolate.

SCENE   II.

A D A M, A N D   E V E.

RECITATIVE.

A D A M.

O Eve ! in evil hour thou didſt give ear
To that falſe worm, of whomſoever taught
To counterfeit man's voice, true in our fall,

                  Falſe

False in our promis'd rifing, fince our eyes
Open'd we find indeed, and find we know
Both good and evil, good loft, and evil got,
Bad fruit of knowledge !

A I R.

"How fhall I behold
"Henceforth or God, or angel, erft with joy,
"And rapture oft beheld? O! might I here
"In folitude live favage, in fome glade
"Obfcur'd, where higheft woods, impenetrable
"To ftar, or fun-light, fpread their umbrage broad,
"And brown as evening. Cover me, ye pines,
"Ye cedars, with innumerable boughs
"Hide me, where I may never fee them more."

RECITATIVE.

Wou'd thou had'ft hearken'd to my words, and
        ftay'd
With me, as I befought thee, when that ftrange
Defire of wand'ring, this unhappy morn,
I know not whence poffefs'd thee ! we had then
                                    Remain'd

Remain'd ftill happy ; not as now defpoil'd
Of all our good, fhamed, naked, mis'rable !

A I R.

" Let none henceforth feek needlefs caufe t' approve
" The faith they owe ; when earneftly they feek
" Such proof, conclude they then begin to fail."

E V E.

Imput'ft thou that to my defire, or will
Of wand'ring, as thou call'ft it, which who knows
But might as ill have happen'd thou being by,
Or to thyfelf perhaps, had'ft thou been there ?
" Was I t' have never parted from thy fide,
" As good have grown there ftill a lifelefs rib.
" Being as I am, why did'ft not thou, the head,
" Command me abfolutely not to go,
" Going into fuch danger as thou faid'ft."
Too facil then, thou did'ft not much gainfay,
Nay, did'ft permit, approve, and fair difmifs.
Had'ft thou been firm, and fix'd in thy diffent,.
Neither had I tranfgrefs'd, nor thou with me.

A D A M.

A D A M.

A I R.

`" Thus it fhall befall
" Him, who to worth in woman overtrufting,
" Lets her will rule ; reftraint fhe will not brook,
" And left t' herfelf, if evil thence enfue,
" She firft his weak indulgence will accufe."

S C E N E   III.

RECITATIVE.

A D A M.

O mis'rable of happy ! Is this the end
Of this new glorious world, and me fo late
The glory of that glory ? who now become
Accurft of bleffed ! Hide me from the face
Of God, whom to behold was then my height
Of happinefs. Yet well, if here wou'd end
The mis'ry ; I deferv'd it, and wou'd bear

I   My

My own defervings; but this will not ferve.

All that I eat, or drink, or fhall beget,

Is propagated curfe. O voice once heard

Delightfully, " Increafe, and multiply."

Now death to hear! For what can I increafe,

Or multiply but curfes on my head,

Heavy! though in their place? O fleeting joys

Of PARADISE, dear bought with lafting woe!

" Did I requeft thee, Maker! from my clay,

" To mould me man? Did I folicit thee

" From darknefs to promote me, or to place

" In this delicious garden? As my will

" Concurr'd not to my being, 'twere but right

" And equal to reduce me to my duft,

" Defirous to refign, and render back

" All I receiv'd,"

E V E.

O ADAM! can I thus behold thee wretched,

Thus mis'rable thro' my default, nor ftrive

To footh thy grief, and foften thy diftrefs?

S   A D A M.

A D A M.

Out of my fight, thou ferpent! that name beft
Befits thee, with him leagu'd, thyfelf as falfe,
And hateful!—

      — — But for thee,
I had continued happy, had not thy pride,
And wand'ring vanity, when leaft was fafe,
Rejected my forewarning, and difdain'd
Not to be trufted; longing to be feen,
Tho' by the Devil himfelf.

A I R,

      "O! why did God,
"Creator wife! that peopled higheft Heav'n
"With fpirits mafculine, create at laft
"This novelty on earth, this fair defect
"Of Nature! and not fill the world at once
"With men, as angels without feminine?"

9   E V E.

E V E.

Forſake me not thus, ADAM! Witneſs Heav'n!
What love ſincere, and rev'rence in my heart
I bear thee, and unweeting have offended,
Unhappily deceiv'd! Thy ſupplicant
I beg, and claſp thy knees; " Bereave me not,
" Whereon I live, thy gentle looks—thy aid—
" Thy counſel in this uttermoſt diſtreſs:
" My only ſtrength, and ſtay! Forlorn of thee,
" Whither ſhall I betake me, where ſubſiſt?"
While yet we live, ſcarce one ſhort hour perhaps,
Between us two let there be peace, both joining,
As join'd in injuries, one enmity
Againſt a foe, by doom expreſs aſſign'd us,
That cruel ſerpent. On me exerciſe not
Thy hatred for this miſery befall'n,
On me already loſt, me than thyſelf
More miſerable: both have ſinn'd, but thou
Againſt God only, I againſt God, and thee:
And to the place of judgment will return,

S 2   There

There with my cries importune Heav'n, that all
The fentence, from thy head remov'd, may light
On me, fole caufe to thee of all this woe,
Me! me! juft object only of his ire.

A D A M.

'Alas! ill able art thou to fuftain
His full wrath, whofe thou feel'ft as yet leaft part,
And my difpleafure bear'ft fo ill.   If pray'rs
Cou'd alter high decrees, I to that place
Wou'd fpeed before thee, and be louder heard,
That on my head all might be vifited,
Thy frailty, and infirmer fex forgiv'n,
To me committed, and by me expos'd.
But rife—Let us no more contend, and blame
Each other, blam'd enough elfewhere, but ftrive
In offices of love, how we may lighten
Each other's burthen in our fhare of woe.
Then to the place repairing, where our Judge
Pronounc'd our doom, there let us both confefs

                                        Humbly

Humbly our faults, and pardon beg, with tears
Wat'ring the ground, and with our fighs the air
Frequenting, fent from hearts contrite, in fign
Of forrow unfeign'd, and humiliation meek.

RECITATIVE ACCOMPANIED.

So fpake our Father penitent, nor EvE
Felt lefs remorfe.   They forthwith to the place
Repairing, where He judg'd them, proftrate fell
Before Him reverent, and both confefs'd
Humbly their faults, and pardon beg'd, with tears
Wat'ring the ground, and with their fighs the air
Frequenting, fent from hearts contrite, in fign
Of forrow unfeign'd, and humiliation meek.

S 3   SCENE

S C E N E   IV.

RECITATIVE.

E V E.

What tidings bring'ſt thou, ADAM! from this new
  gueſt
Angelical, ſo late arriv'd? **Alas!**
My trembling heart forebodes ſome further ill;
For far leſs mild methought his aſpect ſeem'd,
Than RAPHAEL's, ſocial ſpirit! who wont ſo oft
To ſit indulgent with us, and partake
Rural repaſt, permitting us the while
Venial diſcourſe unblam'd.   What tidings? ſay.

A D A M.

Our pray'rs are heard in Heav'n, and Death our due
By ſentence then, when firſt we did tranſgreſs,
Is of his prey defeated many days

                                        Giv'n

Giv'n us of grace, wherein we may repent.

So God appeas'd, from his rapacious claim

Will quite redeem us, and to life reftore.

But longer in this Paradife to dwell,

As not befitting creatures ftain'd with fin,

He fuffers not, but fends us forth to till

The ground from whence he took us, fitter foil!

E V E.

AIR. AFFETUOSO.

" O! unexpected ftroke, worfe than of death!

" Muft I then leave thee, PARADISE, thus leave

" Thee, native foil! Thefe happy walks, and fhades,

" Fit haunt of Gods! where I had hope to fpend

" Quiet, tho' fad the refpite of that day,

" That muft be mortal to us both. O flow'rs!

" That never will in other climate grow,

" My early vifitation, and my laft

" At ev'n, which I bred up with tender hand,

" From the firft op'ning bud, and gave you names,

" Who now fhall rear you to the fun, and rank

S 4   " Your

" Your tribes, and water from th' ambrofial fount ?

" Thee laftly, nuptial bow'r ! by me adorn'd

" With what to fight, or fmell was fweet ; from thee

" How fhall I part, and whither wander down

" Into a lower world, to this obfcure,

" And wild ; how fhall we breathe in other air

" Lefs pure, accuftom'd to immortal fruits ?"

A D A M.

Lament not, Eve ! but patiently refign

What juftly we have loft, nor fet thine heart

Thus overfond on that which is not ours.

Thy going is not lonely—I will guard

Thy fteps from harm, and all thy wants fupply.

E V E.

Adam ! I feel within new life, new hopes

By Heav'n, and thee infpir'd.   Then now lead on,

In me is no delay.   " With thee to go,

" Is to ftay here.   Without thee here to ftay,

" Is to go hence unwilling.   Thou to me

" Art

" Art all things under Heav'n, all places thou!

" Who for my wilful crime art banifh'd hence.".

This further confolation yet fecure

I carry hence—tho' all by me is loft,

Such favour I unworthy am vouchfaf'd,

By me the promis'd Seed fhall all reftore.

So fpake our mother Eve. And Adam heard

Well pleas'd, but anfwer'd not. For now too nigh

The Cherubim advanc'd; and, in their front,

The brandifh'd fword of God before them blaz'd,

Fierce as a comet, which, with torrid-heat,

Smote on that clime, fo late their bleft abode!

Some nat'ral tears they drop'd, but wip'd them foon ;

The world was all before them, where to chufe

Their place of reft, and Providence their guide.

CHORUS. ALLEGRO.

" The world was all before them, where to chufe

"; Their place of reft, and Providence their guide."

To

TO THE

COMPOSER.

THE form of this piece is an Historical
Drama, for this reason, amongst others, viz.
the better to preserve the very words and manner of
MILTON, which must have been frequently alter'd,
and in many instances greatly injur'd by any other
method. The Recitative consequently is of two
kinds, *narrative*, and *interlocutory*. Again, the *narrative* is either *descriptive*, as in Act I. Scene I. and
other places, or else *introductory* to the dialogue, as

Scene

Scene II. and elfewhere. The Compofer will do well to have an eye to thefe diftinctions, as mere *defcription*, or the *introductory narrative* will admit of a different kind of Recitative from the *conver-fation part*; the one being like *painting* in *ftill-life*, the other refembling the *portraits* of *living manners*.

Perhaps he will wifh that the Dialogue contained lefs of the Recitative, and more of the Air, and Chorus. The Compiler however is of opinion that there is a due proportion of each. And if there is lefs opportunity for flourifhes, and repeti-tions, there is more room for fpirited, and fenfible expreffion, to affift the effect of the Dialogue upon the paffions of the hearers, by means of an animated and pathetic Recitative, as well as by a full exertion of the force of mufical language in the Airs, where the length of the performance will but feldom ad-mit of dwelling for a long time together in a dif-play of the minute excellencies of this art.

If

If the Compoſer ſhould think that in ſome places the Recitative is continued too long without the intervention of *Airs*, in this caſe he will find fit places for Airs, beſides what his own judgment will ſuggeſt to him, marked in this manner, page 244, &c.

" I, from the influence of thy looks, receive."

Again. If heſhould think the parts aſſign'd for muſical airs too prolix, in ſome places they may be ſhorten'd, as in the Morning-Hymn, from

Faireſt of Stars laſt in the train of Night,

page 248, to

Made vocal by my ſong, and taught His praiſe,

in page 250.

The Compiler is ſenſible that he ought to make an apology to a Compoſer, for preſuming to interfere ſo much in his province, and he hopes the true reaſon will be accepted as ſuch, viz. that having beſtowed more attention upon this work

ı   than

than it was likely any other perfon would, he thought himfelf capable of pointing out the divifion of it into its feveral parts of Act, Scene, Recitative, Air, Song, Chorus, and the like ; and of fuggefting fome few hints concerning the mufical expreffion in general, though he confeffes himfelf incapable, at the fame time, of executing the moft minute article of it.

F I N I S.

www.ingramcontent.com/pod-product-compliance
Lightning Source LLC
Chambersburg PA
CBHW060553030726
47498CB00005B/1376

9 783744 716284